KT-178-006
MR AND MRS VALANCE
Mum and Dad.
SAMUEL NATHANIEL DANIELS
A top-secret secret agent... from the future.
THE COMMISSIONER
The most HUGELY important person in the Future Perfect Unit.

First published in the UK in 2015 by Usborne Publishing Ltd., Usborne House,
83-85 Saffron Hill, London EC1N 8RT, England. www.usborne.com

Design: Hannah Cobley, Brenda Cole,
Neil Francis and Katharine Millichope.
Editorial: Sarah Stewart and Becky Walker.

A CIP catalogue record for this book is available from the British Library.

FMAMJJASON D/16

ISBN 9781409590477 04065-1

Printed in India

SUPER F.A.R.T.s* versus the MASTER of TIME

By
MATT BROWN

Illustrated by
LIZZIE FINLAY

USBORNE

*Future Agent Recruits in Training

Introducing Compton Valance, his friends and family...

* I know what you're thinking. "Compton Valance" isn't a real name. It's one of those made-up names that sounds a bit funny. Like "Nugget McDoo" or "Basil Burger". But, actually, it is a real name, and it's the name of our main character. And I'm going to tell you why. Well, I'm not, because that would take up a whole extra book. But I am going to tell you how to say it. So after three, say with me... One, two, three:

COM-TON VAAL-AAN-SE – You've got it!

Prologue

The Man With The Silver Mouth

Only three people

in the

WHOLE

UNIVERSE

knew of the existence

of the top-secret file

marked

TOP SECRET – COMPTON VALANCE: TIME CRIME AGENT (IN TRAINING).

Future Perfect Unit Agent, Samuel Nathaniel Daniels.* (When you see *, look at the bottom of the page for an extra note.)

The head of the **FPU**, known only as The Commissioner.

A mysterious man with a strange scar on his face called Susan.**

* Samuel Nathaniel Daniels is an agent in the **Future Perfect Unit (FPU)**, a top-secret government time-travel organization in the future.

** The man's name is Susan, not his scar. The name Susan became a perfectly normal boys' name after it swapped places with Peter in the year 2367.

Neville Breville, the bloke from the **FPU Repair Division** who had to come and show Samuel Nathaniel Daniels how to install the top-secret file on his InfoTab.*

Hang on, that's *four people*, not three people. Alright, there were four people in the WHOLE UNIVERSE who knew of the existence of the top-secret file.

1. Samuel Nathaniel Daniels
2. The Commissioner
3. The man called Susan
4. Neville Breville from the **FPU Repair Division** and his assistant Darren.

* Information Tablet. Every **FPU** agent has their own InfoTab, which is a bit like a handheld computer.

Oh, right, five. There were *five people*, just five, who knew about the file.

1. Samuel Nathaniel Daniels
2. The Commissioner
3. The man with the scar
4. Neville Breville
5. Darren, and Mavis who brings round the teas and coffees every afternoon.

WHAT??? SIX!!!

The point I'm trying to make is that **not many** people knew about the top-secret file.

Wait, let's start again.

Only "*a few*" * people in the WHOLE UNIVERSE knew of the existence of the top-secret file marked

* Better. Non specific. Difficult to verify.

TOP SECRET – COMPTON VALANCE: TIME CRIME AGENT (IN TRAINING).

The reason that so few people knew about the file was because its contents were unbelievably IMPORTANT and tip-top secret. Which is why what was about to happen would come as something of a shock to all concerned.

It was late in the evening on Friday 29th April, 2664, and darkness hung heavy in the unlit corridors of the headquarters of the Future Perfect Unit.

After a long day at work, Samuel Nathaniel Daniels wearily placed his InfoTab into its self-charging Hoverdock.

Then he grabbed his tiny bowler hat from the laser hatstand in the corner of his office and stepped out into **CORRIDOR 7G** to make his way home. As the door closed behind him, a MECHANICAL voice bid him a cheery,

GOODNIGHT, AGENT DANIELS,

SAMUEL NATHANIEL DANIELS

and two seconds later the lights in his office clicked off.

Tap, tap, tap, tap, tap, tap...

The tap, tap, tap of Samuel Nathaniel Daniels's footsteps got quieter and quieter, until soon CORRIDOR 7G was completely

SILENT.

Inside the office, the only illumination was the glow from the TI99 HO-LO-TO-DO that was projected onto the far wall.*

* The TI99 HO-LO-TO-DO is the twenty-seventh century equivalent of a desk calendar and helps FPU agents remember what they have to do that day. HO-LO stands for "holographic" and TO-DO stands for, er, "to-do".

The **TO-DO** list read:

From the desk of
Samuel Nathaniel Daniels
Things To Do Today

- Call **mother** on the **HandPhone***
- Pick up **bowler hat** from cleaners
- **DESTROY** Compton Valance and Bryan Nylon's **disgustingly mouldy** cheese-and-pickled-egg **TIME MACHINE SANDWICH****
- Come up with **BRILLIANT idea** that will make it **look** like I ***didn't*** **forget** to destroy **THE SANDWICH** after all and that everyone thinks is one of the **TOP TEN GREATEST IDEAS** that a human being has **ever had** in the **HISTORY OF THE WORLD*****

* In the twenty-seventh century, phones have advanced a little bit. The *HandPhone* allows you to dial a number on the palm of your hand and then put your thumb in your ear and speak into your little finger. In fact, it's just like the way twenty-first century people make the "*I'll call you*" sign with their hand.

** After Compton Valance and Bryan Nylon accidentally created their own **TIME MACHINE SANDWICH** (and then Bravo, Compton's older brother, had *almost* **DESTROYED THE UNIVERSE** when he stole the **TIME MACHINE SANDWICH**) it had been decided that it would be safest all round if Samuel Nathaniel Daniels **DESTROYED** the **TIME MACHINE SANDWICH**.
He forgot to.

*** After he realized that he *hadn't* **DESTROYED** the **TIME MACHINE SANDWICH**, Samuel Nathaniel Daniels pretended it was because he'd really had a much better idea as to what to do with it. Incredibly, the idea he came up with **WAS** a better idea than simply **DESTROYING THE SANDWICH**. He suggested that as **THE SANDWICH** was the earliest example of a working **TIME MACHINE** <u>EVER</u> discovered, it should be placed in a museum.

A few minutes later, the door to the office s l o w l y squeaked open and through it crept a mysterious figure wearing a l o n g white wig, a curious red coat and a GIGANTIC moustache.

Looking around, the oddly dressed, shadowy figure walked over to the self-charging Hoverdock. Picking up the InfoTab, the figure turned it on and started tapping the screen with great speed until he found what he was looking for: the tip-top secret file marked

He typed in a password and then pushed a small blinking device that he was holding into a slot on the side of the InfoTab.

In a few short moments the file had been copied and the InfoTab placed back in the Hoverdock.

Then, with a quick check around the office to make sure everything was *just* as he had found it, the mysterious figure twiddled his IMMENSE moustache, turned smartly on his heels and left.

As he closed the door and prowled back down the corridor, the mysterious figure smiled – and two rows of sparkling, silver teeth glinted in the darkness.

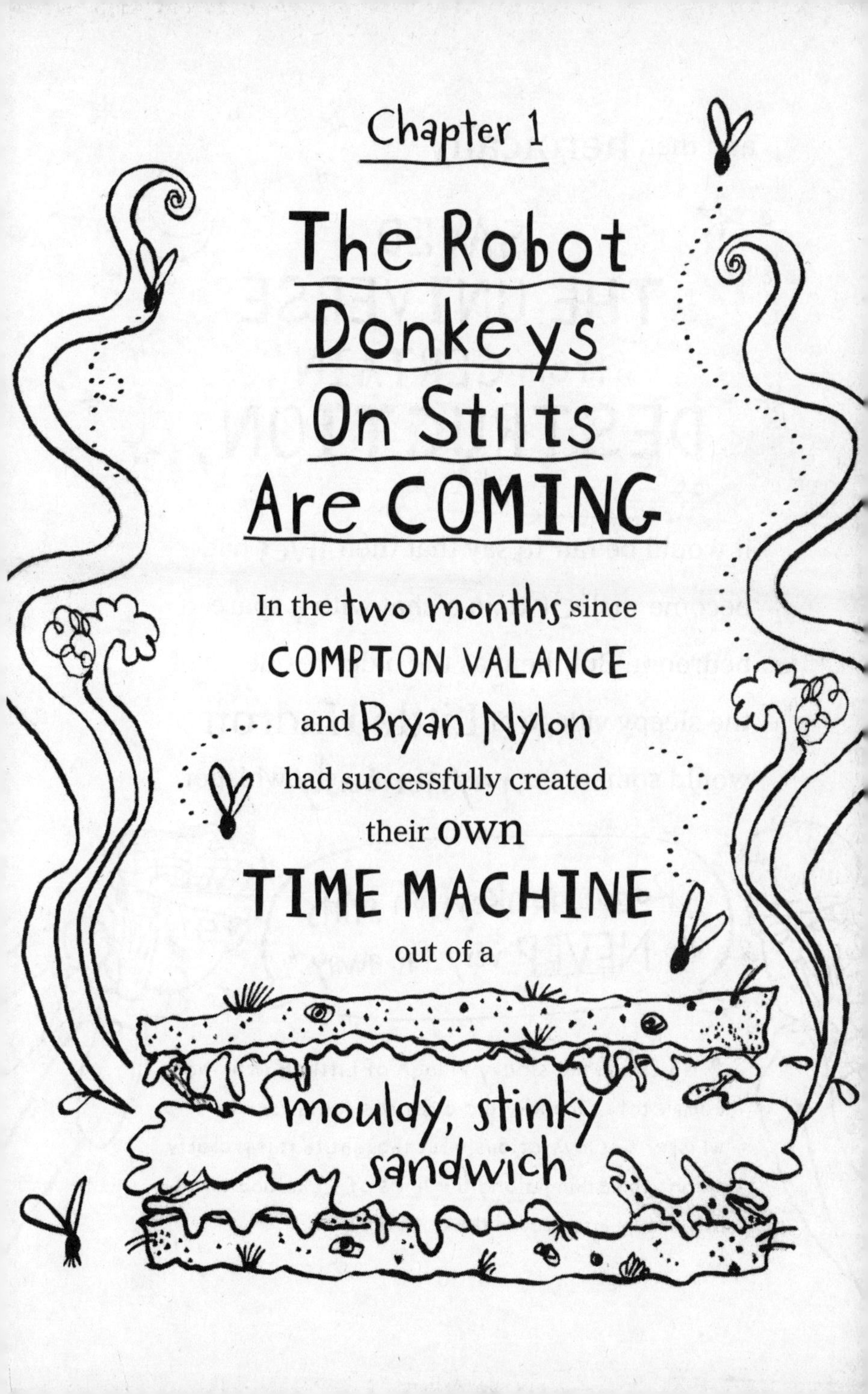

Chapter 1

The Robot Donkeys On Stilts Are COMING

In the two months since COMPTON VALANCE and Bryan Nylon had successfully created their own TIME MACHINE out of a mouldy, stinky sandwich and then heroically

SAVED THE UNIVERSE from CERTAIN DESTRUCTION,

it would be fair to say that their lives had become duller than a chat with a spare bedroom. But then, as the older residents of the sleepy village of Little Hadron would sometimes mysteriously whisper,

Robot donkeys on stilts are NEVER very far away.*

* No one in the sleepy village of Little Hadron was completely sure why the older residents used to whisper this mysteriously but thought that it probably meant something along the lines of, "Exciting times are often just around the corner".

Compton and Bryan had broken up for the summer holidays from St Geoffrey's Junior School exactly one week earlier and made every effort to halt the boredom that was creeping into their lives. They had already tried to knit a bra out of spaghetti.*

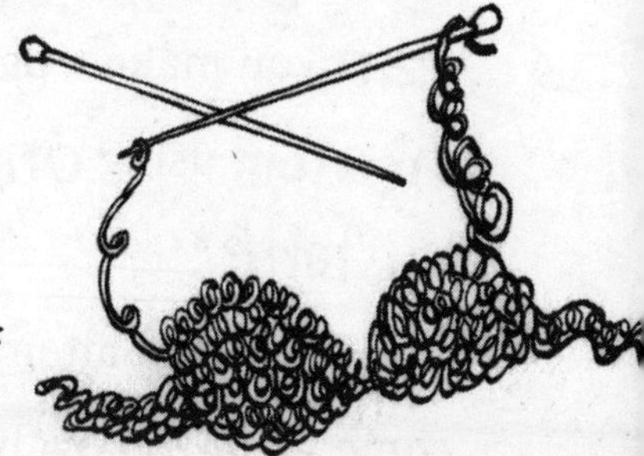

They had attempted to make as many words as possible by using upside-down numbers on a calculator.**

* They couldn't.

** They became very good at this and managed over two hundred words. Compton's favourite was 531608, which when the calculator is turned upside down spells the word "bogies" and Bryan's favourite was 317537, which spells "Leslie". Nobody quite knew why Bryan loved this word so much!

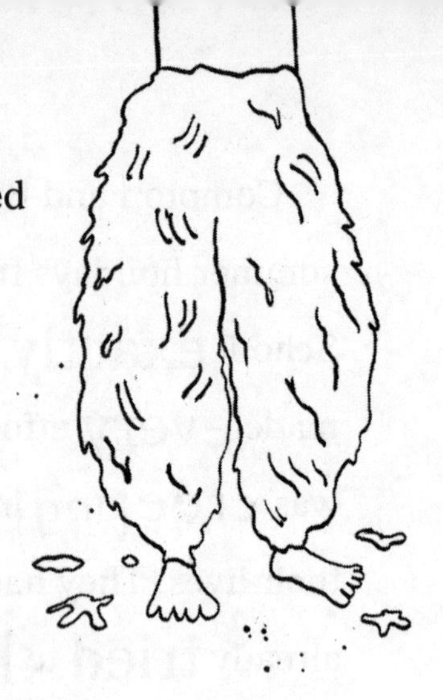

They had even turned their attention to the GREATEST of ALL questions; can you make a pair of trousers using only custard?*

Their latest attempt to pump some adventure back into their lives involved walking around Little Hadron with sieves on their heads, trying to see if they could make contact with aliens.**

* No. Well, at least not *yet*. The first pair of custard trousers would be made by Compton and Bryan but not until the year 2199. (Don't ask. It's a very, very, very long story.)

** Sadly this attempt would be unsuccessful. The first human contact with aliens took place in May 2191 and was something of a disappointment. The alien in question, Reg Halifax from the planet Cantona, only spoke three words of English: "jam", "ocelot" and "toggle". The problem was that no one on earth spoke any Cantonian and so Reg spent most of his stay eating jam and toggling ocelots.

said Compton.

said Bryan, adjusting the coat hanger antenna on his sieve hat.

said Compton, suddenly stopping on the pavement outside the Little Hadron postbox.

Well, said Compton, looking over his shoulder to make sure **no one** could hear.

It's probably **nothing**, but the other day I was in **Feynman's Newsagent** getting some **Lucky Suckers** and a couple of packs of **Sour Flowers**, when all of a sudden I felt **something** on my head. When I turned round there was this weird-looking bloke standing over me, holding a tape measure.

"So, he was measuring your head?" said Bryan slowly.

"Yeah," Compton nodded, thinking just how strange it sounded when it was said out loud. "I think he was."

"Well, now you come to mention it," said Bryan, "something odd happened to me last week too." He paused for a moment. "I was on the bus with my mum going into town," he began. "And I was sitting in my usual seat."

"Second from the back, driver's side?" said Compton.

said Bryan.

"Classic," said Compton, shaking his head and smiling.

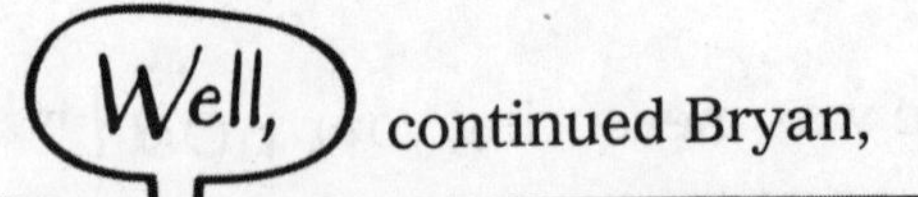

continued Bryan,

there was already a man sitting at the back of the bus. He looked a bit like a businessman but quite a WEIRD one cos he was wearing a really tight black suit and a super-small bowler hat. Anyway, as he passed me to get off the bus, I felt something touch my shoulder, and when I looked there was an empty crisp packet on it.

An empty crisp packet?

said Compton.

"Yes," said Bryan. "An empty crisp packet."

"What flavour?" said Compton.

"Prawn cocktail," said Bryan. "Supermarket own brand!"

"Hmmm," said Compton. "That IS weird."

"Yes, and that's not all," continued Bryan. "Because when I looked back through the window, I saw the man had got off the bus and was standing on the pavement, just looking at me, and then a second later he was gone."

"*Gone?*" said Compton.

"Gone," said Bryan.

"As in?" said Compton.

"Well, just *gone,*" said Bryan again.

"*Gone?*" said Compton again. "Like, *completely?*"

"That's right," said Bryan. "*Completely* gone."

Compton thought for a moment and then nervously looked over his shoulder again.

"The weirdest thing of ALL," Compton said, "is this feeling I've got that we're being WATCHED."

As it turned out, the feeling wasn't such a weird one because behind the bus stop on the other side of the street, a man who wouldn't be born for over five hundred years and who had disguised himself by placing two carrier bags on each foot and a discarded, family-sized fried-chicken bucket on his head, was watching Compton and Bryan through a miniature telescope.

You see, despite the very dull start to their school holidays, **life** in Little Hadron was about to get a whole lot **more** interesting. At that precise moment,

THUNDERING

towards Compton and Bryan was an adventure so exciting and so

ENORMOUS

that it was like... Well, it was like some robot donkeys on stilts had been just around the corner and were about to arrive at any minute.

Chapter 2

No Hat Is Definitely Better Than A Chicken-Bucket Hat

History has forgotten the reason that Samuel Nathaniel Daniels had chosen to get his disguise from the nearest bin. *Perhaps* he had adopted such hopeless camouflage because he had been in a big *hurry* when he'd travelled back in time from the twenty-seventh century to monitor Compton Valance and Bryan Nylon.

Perhaps it was because he didn't have any money as he had left his purse in his other tight silver suit. *Perhaps*, perhaps, *perhaps*.

"Now, where are they?" he muttered impatiently to himself from behind the Little Hadron bus stop.

Samuel Nathaniel Daniels had kept Compton and Bryan in his sights since the beginning of their school holidays. So far, thanks to a series of BRILLIANT disguises that he had assembled from assorted Little Hadron bins, everything had been going to plan.

However, events had **suddenly** taken a **dramatic turn for the worse** because a **rogue** two-day-old **chicken wing** had just decided to fall from the upturned **bucket** on his head and **flop** forwards, rather inconveniently, over the end of his miniature telescope, meaning that he had momentarily lost track of the boys.

exclaimed Compton from behind Samuel Nathaniel Daniels.

The agent spun round quickly.

"Ah, ah, er, er," mumbled Samuel Nathaniel Daniels.

Compton and Bryan had run around the block, across the playground opposite and doubled back on themselves. In doing so they had been able to sneak up behind Samuel Nathaniel Daniels whilst he had been dealing with the "fried chicken incident".

"What's going on?" said Bryan. "Why have you been following us? Er, hello, by the way."

"Er, hello to you too," said Samuel Nathaniel Daniels, trying to take charge of the situation despite the fact that a second rogue chicken wing had appeared from his bucket hat and was flapping about on top of his head.

"Listen, boys! Some very important people need to talk to you about something

EXTRAORDINARILY secret and unbelievably important."

"Okay," said Compton. "What is it?"

"Well, I can't talk about it now," said Samuel Nathaniel Daniels. "We need to wait for the very important people to arrive. Is there somewhere we can meet? Where will you be this afternoon?"

"Well, Dad is taking us for lunch in town later," said Compton. "It's a holiday treat. We're going to this awesome place called The Burger Shack."

Samuel Nathaniel Daniels started furiously tapping on his InfoTab.

"Burger Shack, *Burger Shack*," he muttered as he typed. "Ah, here we are, The Burger Shack. Does it have a top-secret secret office?"

"Erm, no," said Compton.

"Or a highly-secure underground lair?"

"Erm, no," said Compton. "They do have a not-really-very-secret toilet, though?"

"Excellent," said Samuel Nathaniel Daniels. "Let me pull up the construction plans. Great, got them. Ah, I see, the not-really-very-secret-toilet for male human use has four cubicles. Let's meet in the third cubicle at, shall we say, **12.30 p.m.**? *Agreed?*"

"Agreed!" said Compton, smiling at Bryan.

Neither knew precisely what was going to happen but they had spent enough time in the company of Samuel Nathaniel Daniels and the **Future Perfect Unit** to know that whatever it was would be

UNBELIEVABLY,
MIND-BOGGLINGLY,
TOAST-BURNINGLY,
PANT-SCORCHINGLY

EXCITING.

Samuel Nathaniel Daniels looked around to make sure no one was looking and then pushed a button on his **W.A.T.CH.***

* **W**rist **A**ctivated **T**ime **CH**anger, first invented in 2589 to allow the wearer to travel forwards or backwards in time, to any point or place.

"Don't forget," he said. "12.30 p.m.!"

One second later the air around him

crackled and fizzed

and he completely

DISAPPEARED.

One second after that, Samuel Nathaniel Daniels

REAPPEARED

wearing a snorkel, a bathing costume and carrying a GIANT inflatable banana. He looked around in confusion.

said Compton.

said Samuel Nathaniel Daniels.

And with **that** he pushed another button on his **W.A.T.CH.** and

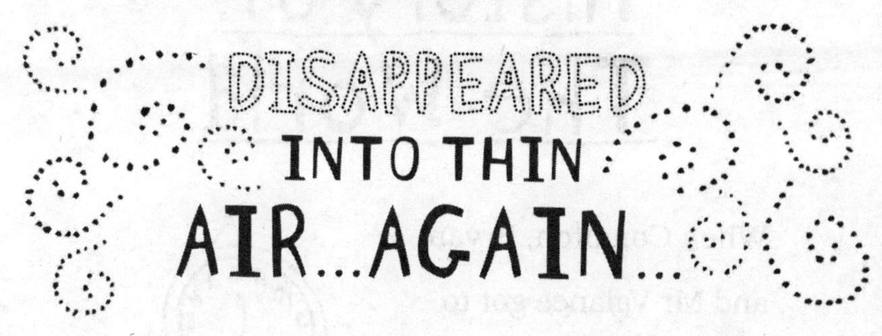

Chapter 3

The Second STRANGEST Sight In The History Of The World

When Compton, Bryan and Mr Valance got to The Burger Shack it was **12.26 p.m.** Not long to wait until Compton and Bryan's super-exciting meeting with Samuel Nathaniel Daniels but still enough time for Compton's dad to perform some of his world famous pre-burger ordering.

"Let's get some spicy chicken wings with barbecue dip, some crispy potato skins and a couple of bowls of onion rings," he said, licking his lips. "That should keep us going while we decide on our burgers."

"Oh," added Mr Valance with a twinkle in his eye. "And how about a round of Zillion-Dollar Milkshakes too?"

Ordinarily the mere mention of a Zillion-Dollar Milkshake, or ZDM as they were more casually referred to, would have had Compton and Bryan whooping and hollering in delight. Each one was made using a super-secret recipe that had been handed down through eleven generations of the same family.*

All that was really known about it was that:

* Legend had it that the creator of the ZDM spent sixteen years in complete isolation in a Buddhist monastery perfecting the recipe and that at least four wars in the last three hundred years had been started in an attempt to get hold of the full list of ingredients.

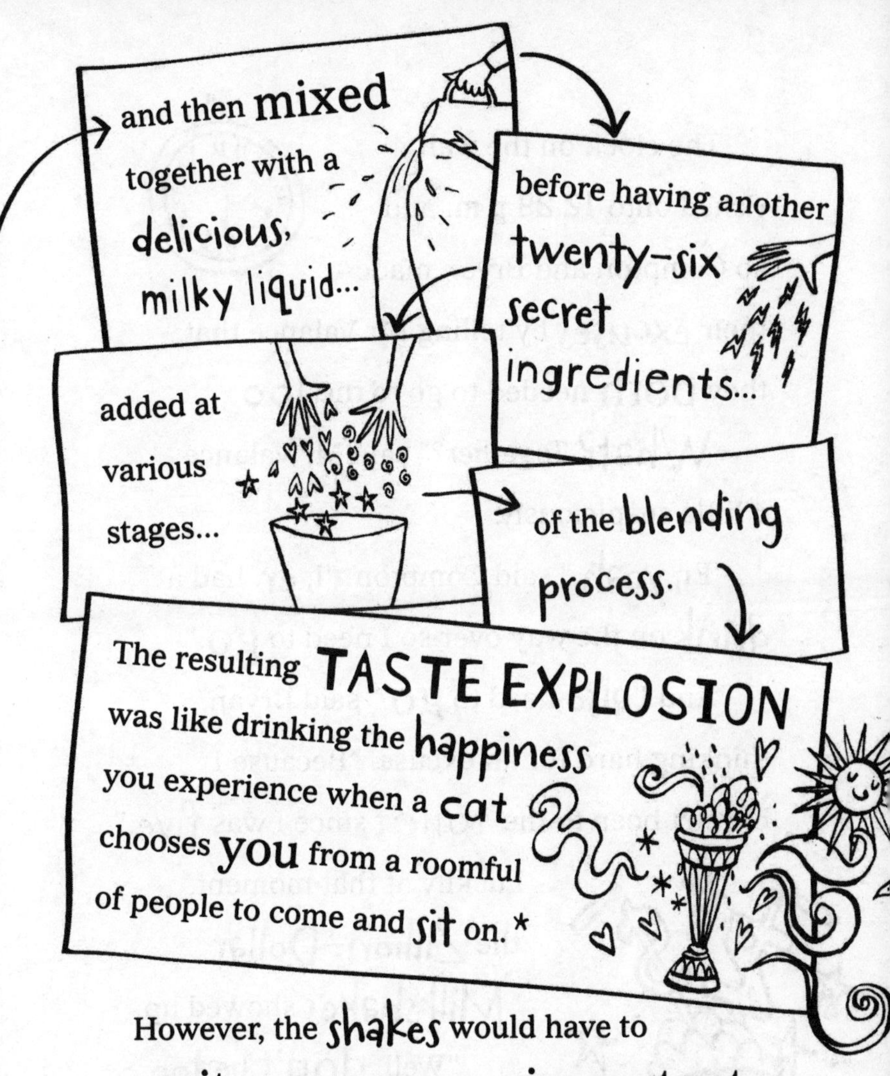

However, the shakes would have to wait, as there were more important matters to attend to.

* Unless of course you dislike cats, in which case it was like the happiness you experience when you're sitting in a car at some traffic lights and you tell yourself that you're going to control the traffic lights with your blinks and the next time you blink, the traffic light changes.

The clock on the wall ticked onto 12.29 p.m. and so Compton and Bryan made their excuses by telling Mr Valance that they both needed to go to the loo.

"What? *Together?*" said Mr Valance a little suspiciously.

"Er, yeah," said Compton. "I, er, had a drink on the way over so I need to go."

"And I also need to go," said Bryan, thinking hard for an excuse. "Because I haven't been to the toilet since I was five."

Luckily at that moment, the Zillion-Dollar Milkshakes showed up.

"Well, don't be too long," Mr Valance said distractedly as he watched beads of condensation trickle down the side of his refrigerated, bejewelled milkshake goblet.

Taking their opportunity, Compton and Bryan hurried off to the toilets. As they did, Compton noticed a strange-looking man sitting on a table by himself in the far corner of The Burger Shack. He was wearing a l o n g overcoat and had a small bowler hat perched on top of his head. He was also reading from a menu that was quite clearly upside down.

The door to the toilets BANGED open, and Compton and Bryan found themselves facing four closed cubicle doors.
Were we supposed to meet in the third cubicle from the left OR the third cubicle from the right?
whispered Bryan.
I can't remember,
whispered back Compton.
Third from the right, I think.

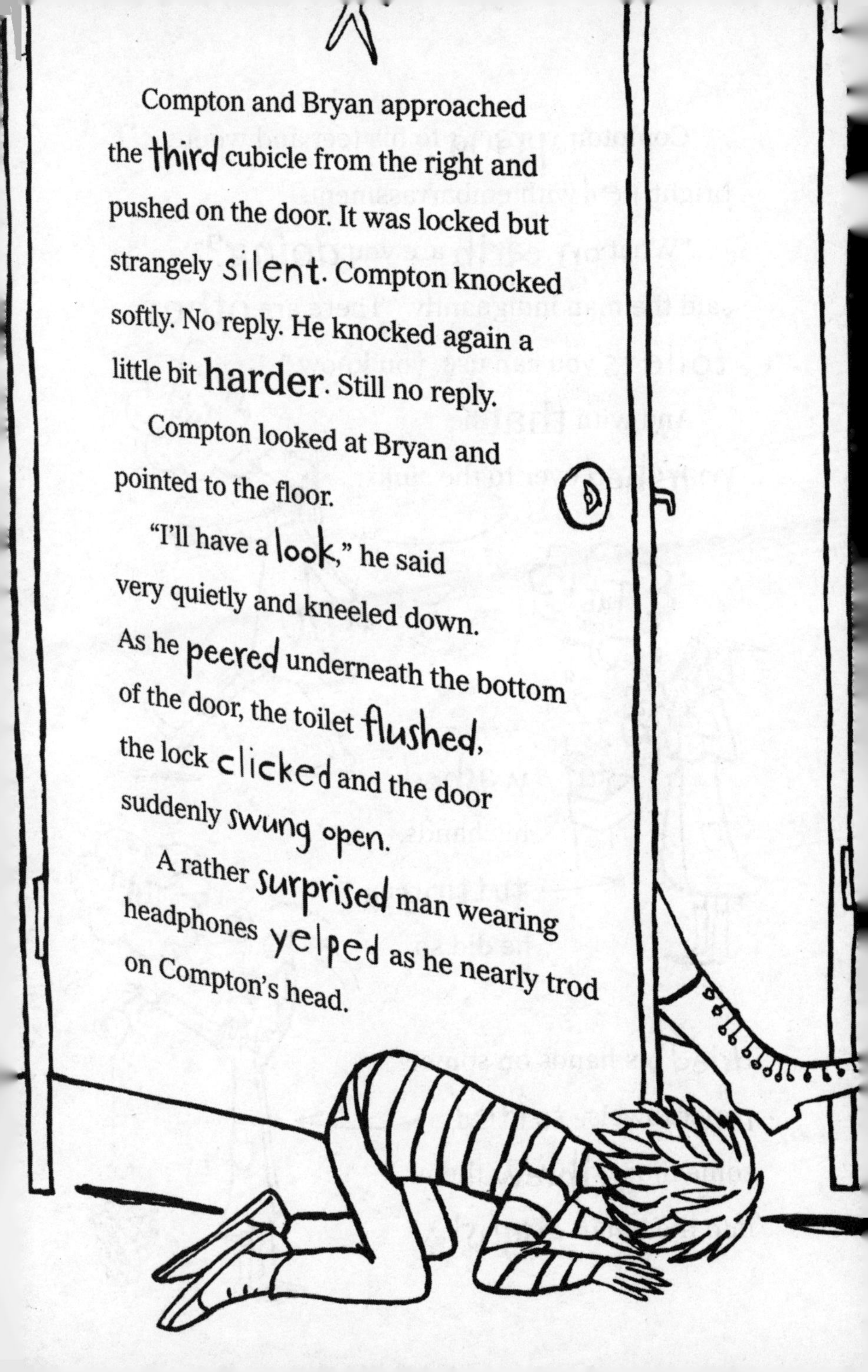

Compton and Bryan approached the **third** cubicle from the right and pushed on the door. It was locked but strangely **silent**. Compton knocked softly. No reply. He knocked again a little bit **harder**. Still no reply.

Compton looked at Bryan and pointed to the floor.

"I'll have a **look**," he said very quietly and kneeled down. As he **peered** underneath the bottom of the door, the toilet **flushed**, the lock **clicked** and the door suddenly **swung open**.

A rather **surprised** man wearing headphones **yelped** as he nearly trod on Compton's head.

Compton sprang to his feet and went bright red with embarrassment.

"What on earth are you *doing?*" said the man indignantly. "There are other toilets you can use, you know."

And with that he marched over to the sinks...

washed his hands, tutting as he did so...

dried his hands on some paper towels, tutted some more, threw them into the bin in disgust...

tutted, turned back and faced Compton and Bryan, opened his mouth to say something, shut his mouth without saying anything, tutted, shook his head, opened his mouth again, shut it again without saying anything, tutted...

and walked out of the toilets, tutting as he left.

Compton looked at Bryan.

"Perhaps we should try the third cubicle from the left," he said.

"That's *probably* a GOOD idea," said Bryan, nodding.

Compton walked over to the **shut** cubicle door and **knocked** sharply. As he did, the door swung slowly open and Compton and Bryan were confronted with the SECOND STRANGEST SIGHT THE WORLD HAD EVER SEEN. *There*, sitting on the closed toilet lid, was *Samuel Nathaniel Daniels*, and sitting on one of his knees was *The Commissioner*

whilst perched on the other knee was a man with a crescent-shaped scar on his face, who was dressed in a tight black suit.*

EXCELLENT, you made it,

grunted Samuel Nathaniel Daniels, standing up and pushing the two human weights off his lap.

I'm SO glad. I don't think my knees could have taken much more of THAT.

* On going to press, the strangest sight the world had ever seen was in 2005 when Wincey Bobbins, an eleven-year-old girl from Kettering, saw a pig playing chess with a horse. I know what you're thinking: "What's so strange about a pig playing chess with a horse?" Well, the pig played a Barnes Opening, which the horse countered with a Hanging Platypus Defence!** You see, I told you it was strange.

** For any non-chess players reading this, a Barnes Opening is where "white" begins by moving the f2 pawn to the f3 space. A Hanging Platypus Defence is where "black" kicks the chessboard with their back legs, knocking all the pieces on the floor!

Compton and Bryan watched as the scar-faced man shuffled out of the gloomy cubicle and into the light. His hair was tightly curled but almost entirely white and his suit was a black version of the one Samuel Nathaniel Daniels wore *except* it had short trousers. This would have looked unusual enough but what made it EXTRA weird was that the scar-faced man was also wearing a pair of silver cowboy boots.

"Compton and Bryan," said Samuel Nathaniel Daniels. "You remember The Commissioner, of course?"

The Commissioner s l o w l y walked out of the cubicle smoothing down her furry orange onesie and running her hand through her mass of dark, wavy hair.

said The Commissioner, grabbing their hands and shaking them.

Once The Commissioner stopped shaking their hands, Samuel Nathaniel Daniels introduced them to the scar-faced man.

"And this," he said, "is Mr Susan Glanville."

* The whole "UNIVERSE GOING KA-BLAMMO" thing that The Commissioner is referring to was when Compton's older brother Bravo stole the TIME MACHINE SANDWICH. He went back in time so often and changed the past in such a way that the last time The Commissioner had seen Compton and Bryan was when THE UNIVERSE only had one second before it EXPLODED. Thankfully for all concerned, Compton and Bryan's quick thinking saved the day.

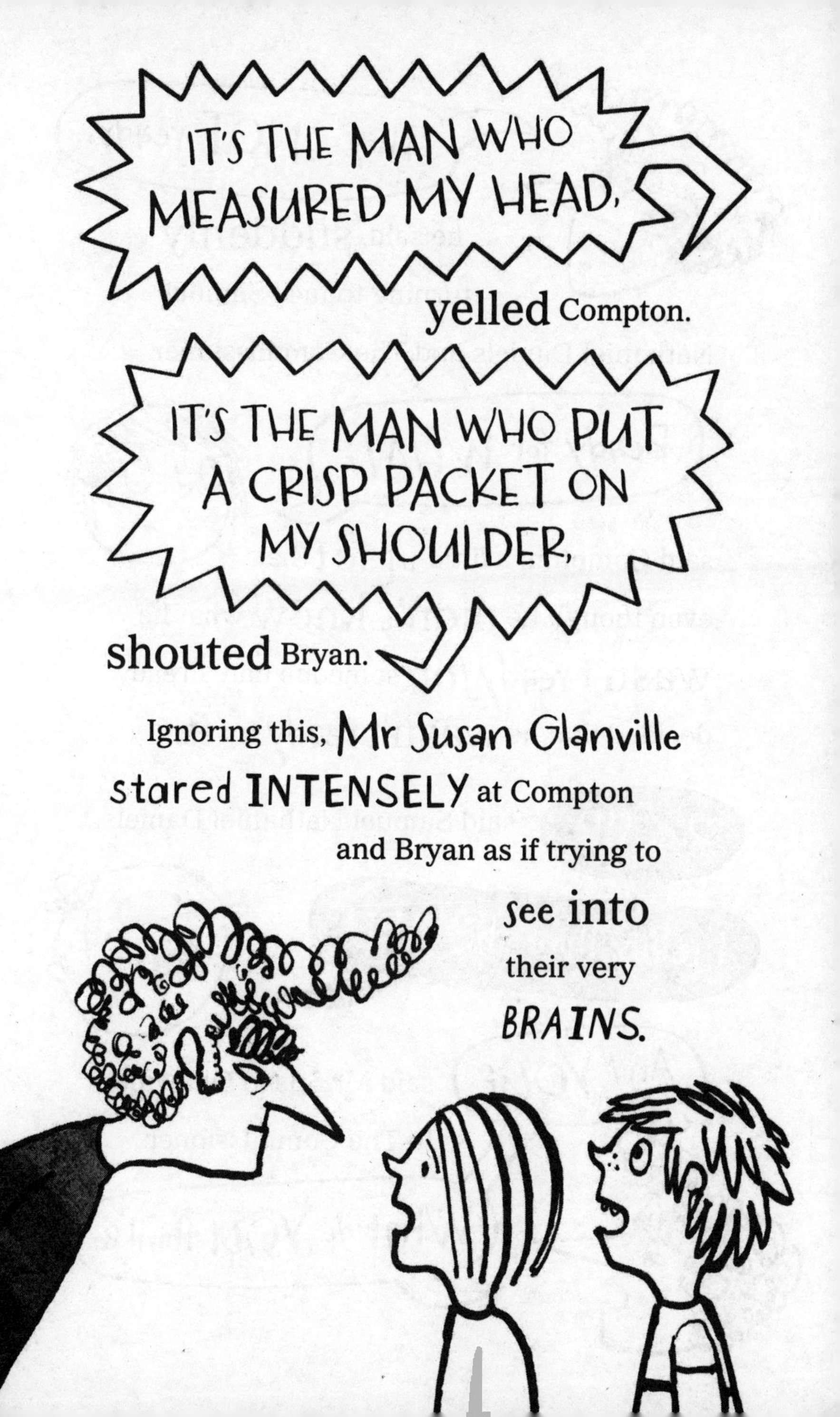

"IT'S THE MAN WHO MEASURED MY HEAD," yelled Compton.

"IT'S THE MAN WHO PUT A CRISP PACKET ON MY SHOULDER," shouted Bryan.

Ignoring this, Mr Susan Glanville stared **INTENSELY** at Compton and Bryan as if trying to see **into** their very ***BRAINS***.

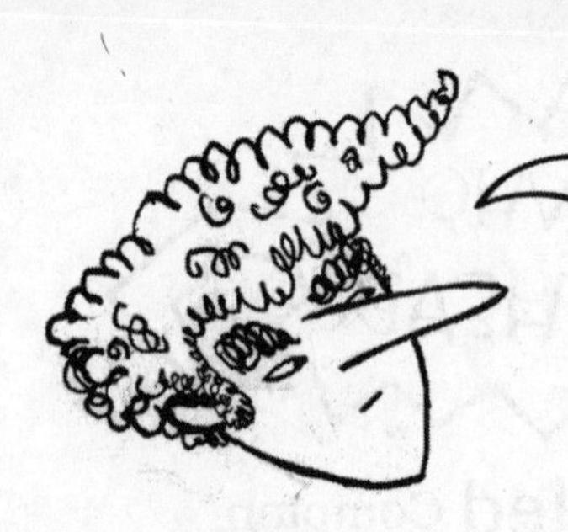

They're NOT ready,

he said, **suddenly** turning to face Samuel Nathaniel Daniels and The Commissioner.

Ready for WHAT?

said Compton, a *little* upset that even though he **didn't know** what he **wasn't ready *for*,** someone had already decided that he **wasn't ready** for ***it.***

But, SIR,

said Samuel Nathaniel Daniels.

I really think they ARE.

And YOU?

said Mr Susan Glanville to The Commissioner.

What do YOU think?

The Commissioner nodded.

she said.

Bryan chimed in, only a little bit louder.

Mr Susan Glanville turned towards him, his eyes BURNING like fires.

he said mysteriously.

Chapter 4

The Truth About Mr Susan Glanville

"Mr Susan Glanville," explained Samuel Nathaniel Daniels in his most serious voice, "is one of the most cunning agents ever to work within the FPU. He has been awarded the CM *sixteen* times,* the CMWCM *twelve* times,** the CMWCMWMOC *four* times,*** and he is the longest-*ever* serving head of the F. A. R. T. Academy."

* Commendation Medal.

** Commendation Medal Winner's Commendation Medal.

*** Commendation Medal Winner's Commendation Medal Winner's Medal Of Commendation.

Samuel Nathaniel Daniels paused dramatically. Compton and Bryan looked at each other and burst out laughing.

HA HA HA HA, HAH HA HA...

The Fart Academy?

spluttered Compton.

There's a place where you teach people HOW to fart?

Can students specialize in different types of farts?

laughed Bryan.

Like wettest guff and most silent-but-deadly?

Once you've graduated from the Fart Academy do you go on to pee-ewwniversity?

asked Compton.

Mr Susan Glanville narrowed his eyes. Samuel Nathaniel Daniels shuffled from side to side awkwardly.

"F-A-R-T," he said, spelling out each letter slowly and deliberately. "It stands for Future Agent Research and Training. It's where anyone who wants to be an agent for the FPU begins their training."

The boys suddenly stopped laughing.

"You mean," said Bryan, "there's a school where you can learn how to become a TIME-TRAVELLING agenty thingy for the FPU? Just like you are?"

Samuel Nathaniel Daniels nodded and smiled.

"That's right," said The Commissioner. "And for the last few weeks Mr Susan Glanville has been assessing you two, with the assistance of Samuel Nathaniel Daniels, to see if you could become part of the training program at the F. A. R. T. Academy."

Compton and Bryan's eyes widened with excitement.

"*However,*" said Mr Susan Glanville sharply, "to take two ten year olds would require the candidates to be of the HIGHEST *possible* standard and so far I haven't been very impressed with what I have seen."

"What?" said Compton. "But we'd be great time-travely agenty thingies. I mean, we...we...we invented a

TIME MACHINE!"

"Pah," snorted Mr Susan Glanville as he walked over to the hand basins and preened his hair in the mirror.

"That was pure luck. You failed both the head-measuring exercise and the Trial By Crisp Packet On The Shoulder. My grandmother could have done better on those. NO, NO, NO. Such a failure will not do."*

The smiles fell from Compton and Bryan's faces. The Commissioner walked up behind Mr Susan Glanville and put her hand on his shoulder.

"Susan," she said gently. "They saved THE UNIVERSE. Just the two of them. When all hope seemed lost, and most of us were panicking, they came up with the

* It is a closely guarded FPU secret as to what you can tell about a person by measuring their head or placing an empty prawn cocktail crisp packet on their shoulder. All I can tell you is that they reveal a lot!

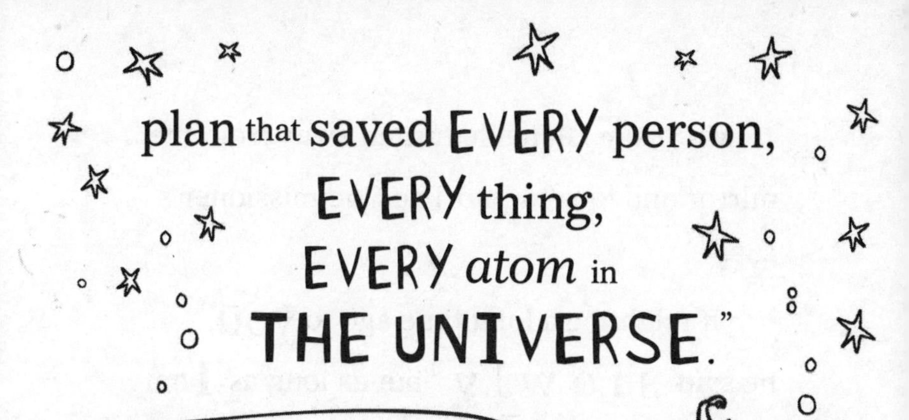

plan that saved EVERY person,
EVERY thing,
EVERY *atom* in
THE UNIVERSE."

Need I remind you what happened the last time a ten year old was accepted into the **F. A. R. T. Academy**?

snapped Mr Susan Glanville, rubbing the scar on his cheek.

"That was a **long** time ago, Susan," said The Commissioner, shaking her head.

Mr Susan Glanville turned away from the mirror and looked into The Commissioner's eyes.

"It might be a long time ago to **you**," he said s l o w l y, "but as long as **I** am in charge of the **Academy**, **I** will make sure **nothing** like **THAT** ever happens again."

He opened up The Commissioner's hand and placed something inside.

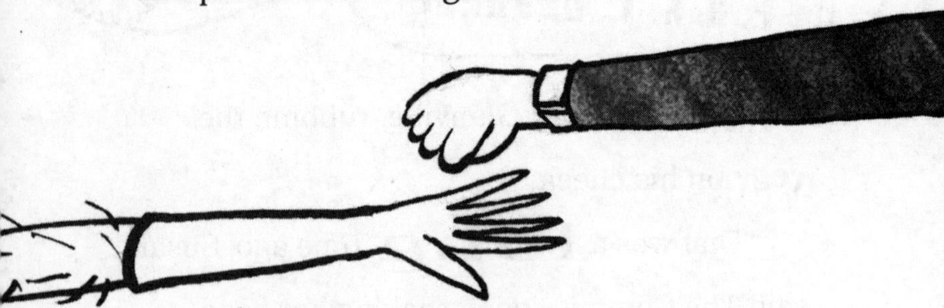

"But," Mr Susan Glanville said with a sigh, walking back into the toilet cubicle, "**you** are **The Commissioner** of the **FPU**, not me. I will accept whatever decision you make. I only hope you know what you are doing."

And with that, Mr Susan Glanville pushed a button on his **W.A.T.CH.** and

DISAPPEARED.

As the air in the cubicle crackled and fizzed, Compton looked nervously at Bryan.

"Crikey," he said. "What's his problem? WHY is he SO cross?"

"It's complicated," said Samuel Nathaniel Daniels. "Mr Susan Glanville has overseen the training of new agents for a *very* **long** time. Under his supervision some of the most brilliant minds have graduated from the **Academy**. Except—"

He paused and glanced at The Commissioner who looked back and nodded.

"Except, a **long** time ago," he continued, "one ten-year-old student thought he was TOO important, TOO clever, TOO powerful. He turned out to be a whole lifetime of TROUBLE."

But that is ALL in the past,

interrupted The Commissioner.

And I can promise that we are taking EVERY measure we can to ENSURE that it NEVER HAPPENS AGAIN.

She turned and faced Compton and Bryan.

"Compton Valance and Bryan Nylon, if *anyone* deserves a chance to come and work for the **FPU**, it's you two. Do you swear to uphold the values of the **Future Perfect Unit**?"

"What are the values of the **FPU**?" whispered Bryan to Compton.

"Rushing around and being weird, I think," whispered Compton, smiling.

Bryan laughed.

"Is there a problem?" said The Commissioner. "Will you uphold the values of the **FPU**?"

"Er, yes," sniggered the boys together.

"Then it gives me GREAT PLEASURE," said The Commissioner, throwing her long, wavy hair behind her as she bent down and pinned a gold badge on Compton and on Bryan, "to invite you both to take part in **PHASE ONE TRAINING** at the **F. A. R. T. Academy**."

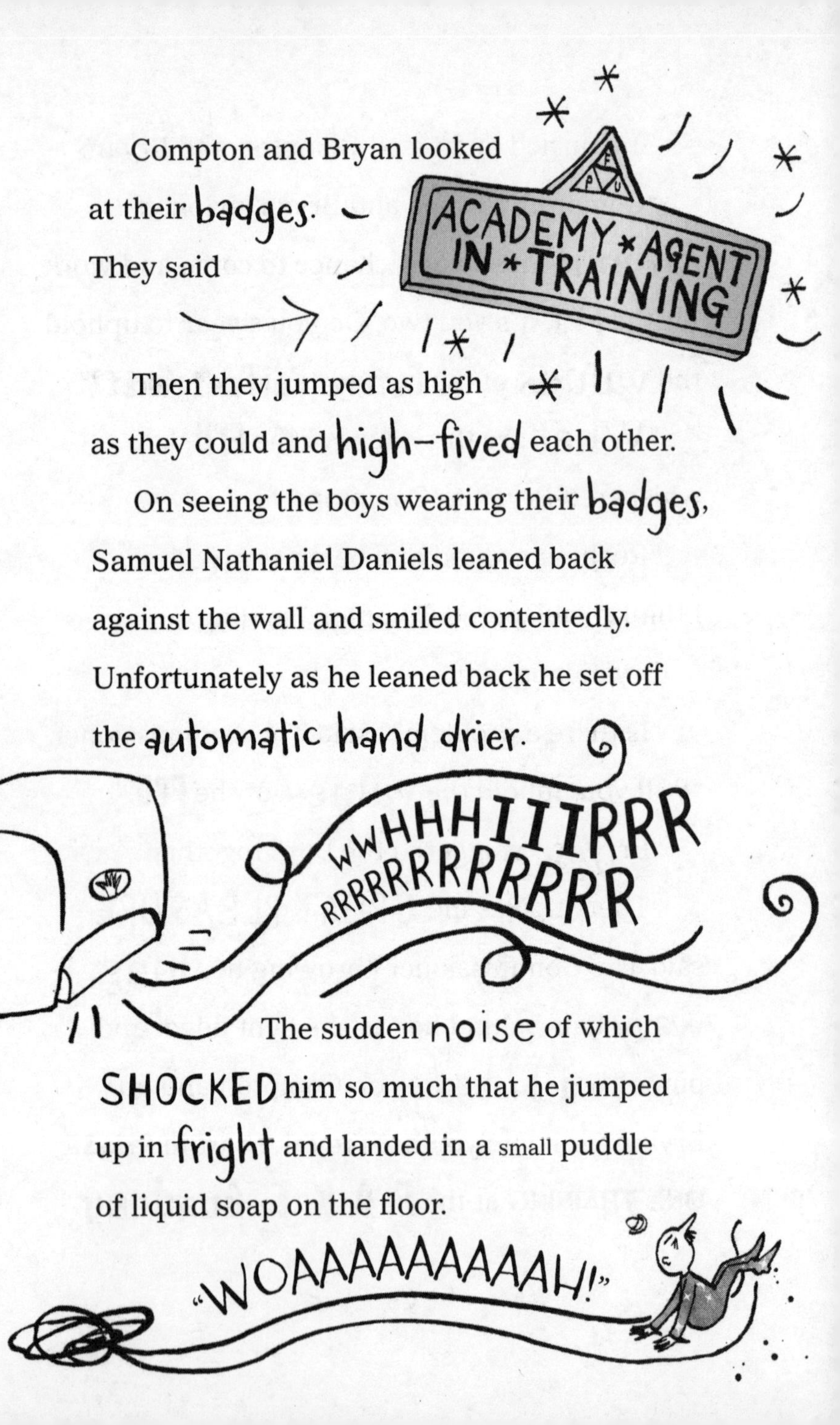

Compton and Bryan looked at their badges. They said

Then they jumped as high as they could and high-fived each other.

On seeing the boys wearing their badges, Samuel Nathaniel Daniels leaned back against the wall and smiled contentedly. Unfortunately as he leaned back he set off the automatic hand drier.

The sudden noise of which SHOCKED him so much that he jumped up in fright and landed in a small puddle of liquid soap on the floor.

He *skidded* on the soap and **smashed** into a **large metal bin** in the corner of the room.

Used paper towels scattered over the toilet floor like **horrible, smelly confetti.**

Not that Samuel Nathaniel Daniels could see because he was *slumped* in the corner of the room with a **bin** on his head.

The Commissioner rolled her eyes.

"Can I leave the formalities to you, Agent Daniels?" she said frostily as she stepped into the toilet cubicle. "Seeing as you're such a SHINING EXAMPLE of what the FPU can achieve." Then, pushing a button on her W.A.T.CH. she turned to Compton and Bryan and gave them a wink.

"Good luck, boys," she smiled. "I shall be keeping a close eye on you."

Once again the air crackled and fizzed and The Commissioner DISAPPEARED.

Samuel Nathaniel Daniels picked himself up and dusted himself off.

"No time to lose," he said. "You can begin your training at once. You will come and stay at the Academy for the next three months."

"*Three months?*" said Compton.

"But school here starts again in a few weeks. And what about my family? I'm not sure they'll let me go off with a total stranger from the twenty-seventh century, even if he is a TIME TRAVELLER."

Samuel Nathaniel Daniels tapped the side of his nose.

"Don't worry," he said, smiling. "We can return you to any TIME we want. For example, we could bring you back to this very moment. To anyone in the twenty-first century it will appear as though no TIME has passed at all. Your mum and dad will NEVER even know you've been away. At the Academy you'll live, breathe, sleep and eat TIME TRAVEL. And then at the end of your PHASE ONE TRAINING, there's a big graduation ceremony. It's magnificent, it really is. Everyone gets a certificate and then there's a huge feast and music and..."

Samuel Nathaniel Daniels let his thoughts trail off and suddenly began to examine his nails.

"However, if you DON'T want to come to the twenty-seventh century and try to become a top-secret secret agent RACING around through TIME and space catching time crims*, then you *only* have to say."

Compton and Bryan looked at each other.

"We're IN," said Compton.

"Too right," said Bryan.

After the boring summer they'd had, there was no way they were going to miss out on this.

"Right," said Samuel Nathaniel Daniels, tapping some buttons on his **W.A.T.CH.**

* A "time crim" is a person who travels through time without the permission of the FPU.

"Let's go then."

And with that, the three of them squeezed back into the third cubicle from the left and shut the door. A moment later the air inside the men's toilets of The Burger Shack crackled and fizzed, and Compton, Bryan and Samuel Nathaniel Daniels

DISAPPEARED.

In the restaurant, Mr Valance had slurped the last of his Zillion-Dollar Milkshake and was becoming a bit concerned about where Compton and Bryan had got to. So, putting down his menu, he pushed back his chair and started walking towards the toilets. The man in the long overcoat and tiny bowler hat started tapping furiously on an InfoTab.

Mr Valance reached the toilets and pushed open the door to go inside. It was empty and quiet. *TOO* EMPTY. *TOO* QUIET.

"Er, *hello?*" he said nervously. "Compton? Bryan? Are you *there*?"

He walked s l o w l y over to the cubicles, and as he did so Compton and Bryan almost fell out of the third one from the left.

"Compton," said his father, looking very strangely at the pair of them.

"Are you guys okay? Where are your clothes? What are you doing in those weird red onesies?"

Compton looked at his father and nearly burst into tears. He grabbed and hugged him as hard as he could.

"Dad," he said, gripping him tightly. "It's so good to see you again."

"*Again?*" said Mr Valance, letting the hug go and looking at his son. "You've only been GONE for a few minutes."

"Oh, er, yes," said Compton nervously. "Yes, that's right – a *few minutes!*"

Chapter 5

A Few Minutes Earlier

"Right," said Samuel Nathaniel Daniels, tapping some buttons on his **W.A.T.CH.** "Let's go then."

And with that, the three of them squeezed back into the third cubicle from the left and shut the door.

A moment later the air inside the men's toilets of The Burger Shack crackled and fizzed, and Compton, Bryan and Samuel Nathaniel Daniels

DISAPPEARED.

When the air around them stopped crackling and fizzing, Compton and Bryan found themselves in a vast, eyeball-achingly white hall. A big sign high up on the wall announced that they were now in

ARRIVALS

They had materialized onto one of a series of black and white circles and as they watched, other people crackled and fizzed into view on the circles around them.

On the far side of the hall were rows of desks.

"*Where* are we?" said Bryan as he watched another silver-suited **FPU** agent and a rather nervous boy materialize four circles down.

"Is *this* the **FPU**?"

said Samuel Nathaniel Daniels, throwing his arms out dramatically,

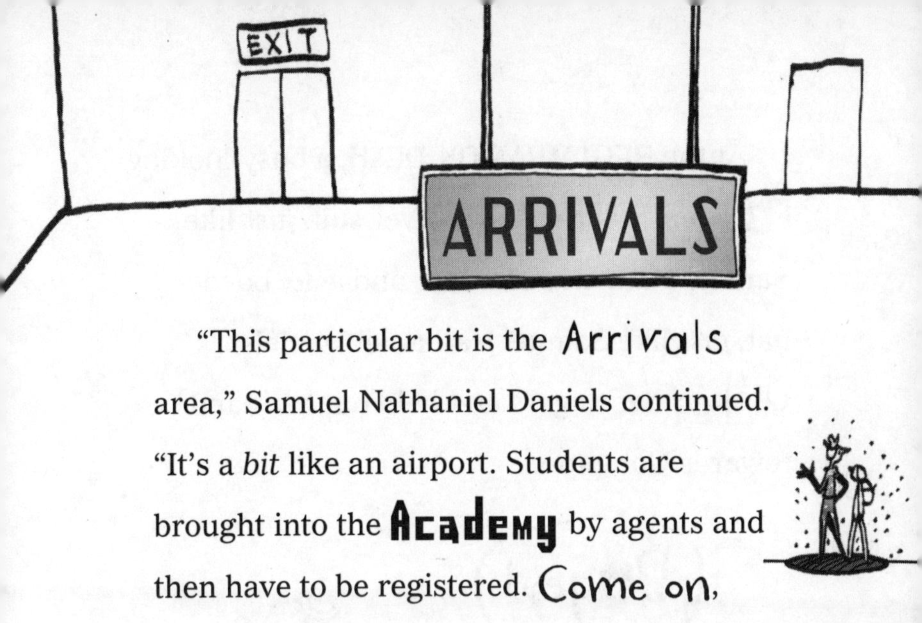

"This particular bit is the Arrivals area," Samuel Nathaniel Daniels continued. "It's a *bit* like an airport. Students are brought into the **Academy** by agents and then have to be registered. Come on, let's get you two signed up."

At the **REGISTRATION DESK**, a busy-looking **FPU** agent wearing a tight silver suit, *just* like Samuel Nathaniel Daniels, and a tiny bowler hat, *just* like Samuel Nathaniel Daniels, clicked her fingers and held out her hand towards Compton.

she said sharply.

Compton looked at Samuel Nathaniel Daniels, who mimed a nose-picking action and nodded towards the FPU agent's outstretched hand.

"BOGEY RECOGNITION TECHNOLOGY," he said by way of explanation.*

"In her *hand?*" said Compton in disgust.

Samuel Nathaniel Daniels nodded.

"Come on, come on," demanded the **FPU** agent, clicking her fingers again. "I haven't got ALL day."

* BOGEY RECOGNITION TECHNOLOGY (BRT) is a twenty-seventh century technological marvel. Every person has their own unique snot pattern, which is almost impossible to copy and so, in order to maintain the highest levels of security, a system of detecting a person's identity from their nose candies was developed.

Compton put his FINGER up his NOSE and had a good root around until eventually he found a splendid, ripe bogey and wiped it on the FPU agent's hand.

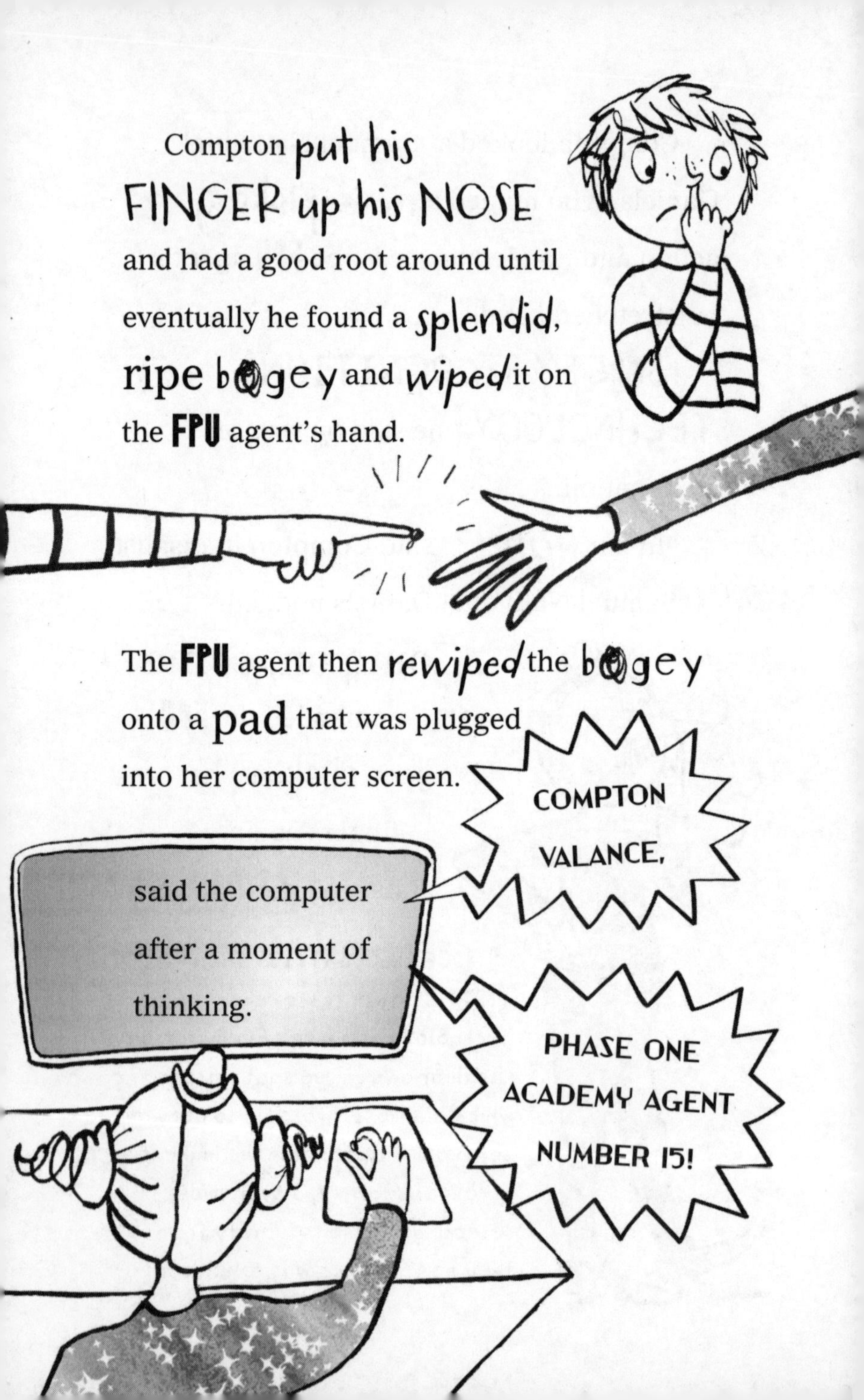

The FPU agent then rewiped the bogey onto a pad that was plugged into her computer screen.

said the computer after a moment of thinking.

HOW does it know who I am?

said Compton.

I didn't know it knew my snot pattern.

I, er, grabbed some last week,

said Samuel Nathaniel Daniels.

When I had you under surveillance.

HOW? said Compton.

Well, I waited until you were asleep,

explained Samuel Nathaniel Daniels,

and simply executed a LEVEL 10 BRP.

BRP?
said Compton suspiciously.
What's a BRP?
Bogey Removal Procedure,
said Samuel Nathaniel Daniels.
I simply used a digit to create an angle of forty-nine degrees and then inserted it into your anterior nares, flexing and rotating to complete a perfect RHINOTILLEXIS.
YOU picked MY nose while I was asleep?
said Compton.

"Correct," said Samuel Nathaniel Daniels. "And then I entered the nasal mucous into our database."

Compton felt a little bit sick.

"C-Compton V-Valance." The FPU Agent had been staring at the two of them during this exchange, but now butted in. "THE Compton Valance?"

"That's right," said Samuel Nathaniel Daniels. "And this is Bryan Nylon."

The FPU Agent's jaw nearly hit the desk.

"B-B-Bryan Nylon," she stammered.

The FPU Agent stood staring at Compton and Bryan with a kind of dreamy, faraway look in her eyes.

"Er, would you like one of my bogeys too?" said Bryan, as much to break the awkward silence as anything.

"Sorry?" said the FPU Agent, still gazing into Bryan's eyes.

Bryan shoved his finger up his nose, had a rootle and pulled out a bogey. He smiled and nodded encouragingly as he held it out towards the FPU Agent.

Without breaking her gaze, the FPU Agent took Bryan's bogey in her own hands and wiped it on the pad next to her computer.

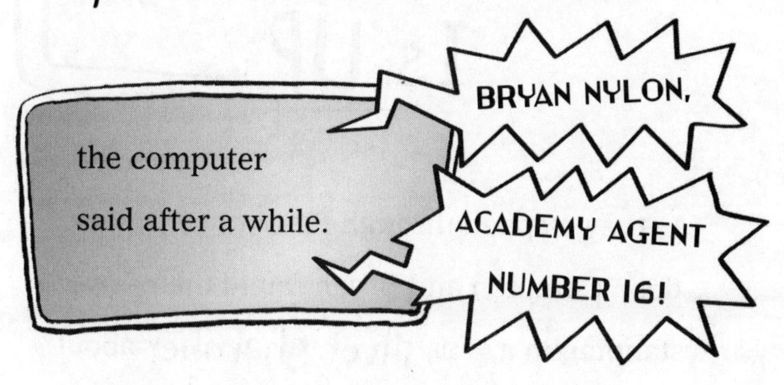

"Right," said Samuel Nathaniel Daniels. "Now that's done and dusted we can get you settled in. Let's get off to your living quarters."

And with that he ushered Compton and Bryan to the Arrivals exit.

"Compton Valance and Bryan Nylon," said the FPU Agent, staring at the hand that Bryan's bogey had been in. "I *can't believe* I had *their* bogeys on *my* finger! I'm NEVER going to wash AGAIN!"

Chapter 6
The Only Way Is UP

As they stepped through the Arrivals exit door, Compton and Bryan found themselves standing in a small, silver chamber about the size of a lift. Looking up, Compton could see that the chamber was SO HIGH that he couldn't even see the roof.

On the wall in front of them was a series of buttons numbered one to ten.

1 2 3 4 5 6 7 8 9 10

"Right then," said Samuel Nathaniel Daniels. "Before we enter the main F. A. R. T. Academy building, we just have to go through a small screening process to make sure that we're not breaking any LAWS OF TIME."

"Like the security you have to go through in an airport?" said Bryan.

"Exactly," said Samuel Nathaniel Daniels, nodding. "So, a couple of quick questions first. Do either of you have a fear of heights, going UNBELIEVABLY fast, or tubes?"

"Er, no," said Compton. "*Why?*"

Samuel Nathaniel Daniels smiled and pushed the third button on the wall.

Compton and Bryan suddenly heard a kind of whooshing noise coming from above them.

Shh-wooooooosssssshh...

Craning their heads back they watched as three clear, human-sized tubes descended from the ceiling and plopped over each of them.

THEN THERE'S ABSOLUTELY NOTHING TO WORRY ABOUT,

shouted Samuel Nathaniel Daniels from inside his tube.

Pay NO ATTENTION to the flashing lights, it's just the FPU computer giving you a quick scan.

But ABOVE ALL just relax and enjoy the ride, we haven't had a REALLY SERIOUS ACCIDENT in here in months.

Compton gulped and looked at Bryan who was staring straight ahead, paralysed with fear. Suddenly he felt a *rush* of air around him and

WWWOOOOOOSSSSSHHHHH!!!

Compton shot off through the tube at a TREMENDOUS *SPEED*.

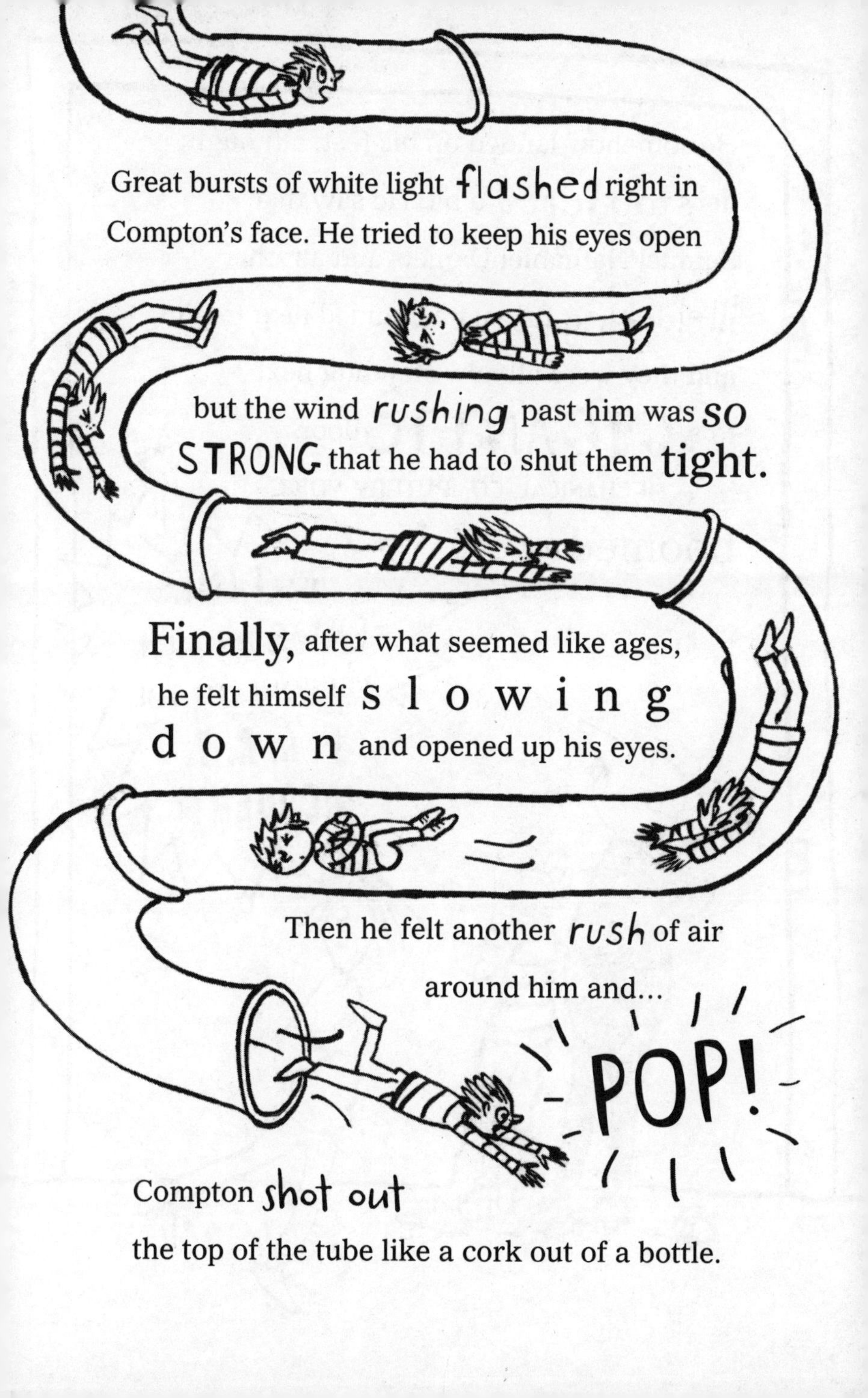

Great bursts of white light flashed right in Compton's face. He tried to keep his eyes open

but the wind rushing past him was SO STRONG that he had to shut them tight.

Finally, after what seemed like ages, he felt himself s l o w i n g d o w n and opened up his eyes.

Then he felt another rush of air around him and...

POP!

Compton shot out the top of the tube like a cork out of a bottle.

He somehow landed on his feet, although he staggered a bit. He saw that Samuel Nathaniel Daniels and a rather ill-looking Bryan had landed next to him, and they were all now standing next to a GIGANTIC door.

A MECHANICAL COMPUTERY VOICE boomed out,

WARNING

WHAT YOU ARE
ABOUT TO READ
MIGHT BE THE
MOST DISGUSTING
THING YOU HAVE
EVER READ
IN YOUR LIFE.
ANYONE OF A
NERVOUS
DISPOSITION
SHOULD SKIP AHEAD
TO CHAPTER 8
IMMEDIATELY.

ANOTHER WARNING

SERIOUSLY,

THIS

IS YOUR

LAST

CHANCE!

Chapter 7

BOGEY RECOGNITION TECHNOLOGY Goes Too Far This Time

The **F. A. R. T. Academy** door opened into a **long**, BRIGHT, white corridor, and Compton and Bryan followed as Samuel Nathaniel Daniels marched off down it.

"Now I imagine this will all seem a *little* unusual," he said as he walked. "But it's really very simple."

Compton looked at Bryan and smiled excitedly. He couldn't BELIEVE he was standing in the twenty-seventh century and about to start training to be an FPU agent.

"The F. A. R. T. Academy is broken down into three classes of students," Samuel Nathaniel Daniels continued. "PHASE ONE, PHASE TWO and PHASE THREE. Each PHASE has their own Rest Zone and Rec Zone."

"What are those?" said Bryan, his eyes goggling with wonder.

"Well, the Rest Zone is where you sleep," said Samuel Nathaniel Daniels. "And the Rec Zone is where you can hang out and relax."

"Cool," said Bryan.

"Students generally enter the Academy between the ages of twelve and thirteen," continued Samuel Nathaniel Daniels. "And only after they have demonstrated some kind of exceptional ability that we think will make them BRILLIANT FPU agents."

"Like saving THE UNIVERSE from certain DESTRUCTION?" said Bryan, smiling.

Er, yes, said Samuel Nathaniel Daniels.

When they had reached THE END of the doorless corridor, Samuel Nathaniel Daniels pushed on the wall ahead and a small drawer *whirred* open. He *plucked* a good, *ripe bogey* from his nose and put it in the drawer. The drawer then *whirred* closed and after a few moments *three green lights* appeared on the wall in front of them. Suddenly a door, which up until that **exact** second had been **completely** INVISIBLE, s l o w l y *hissed* open.

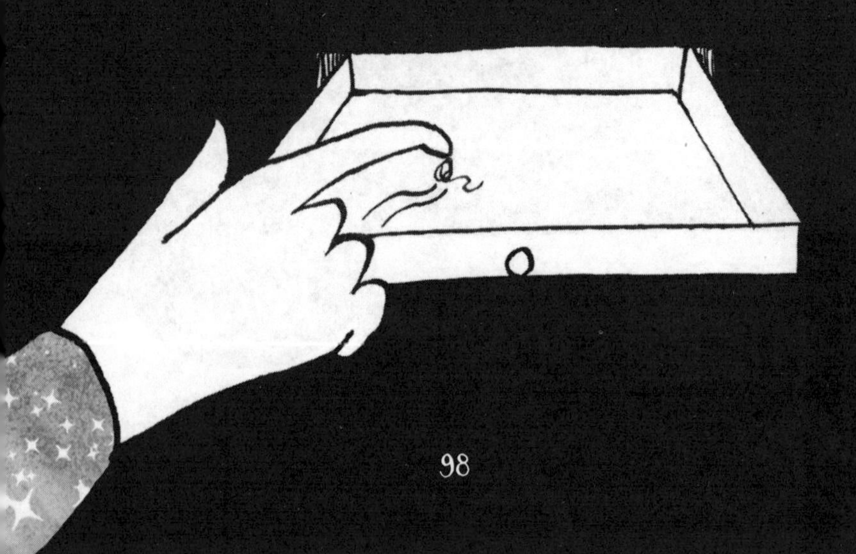

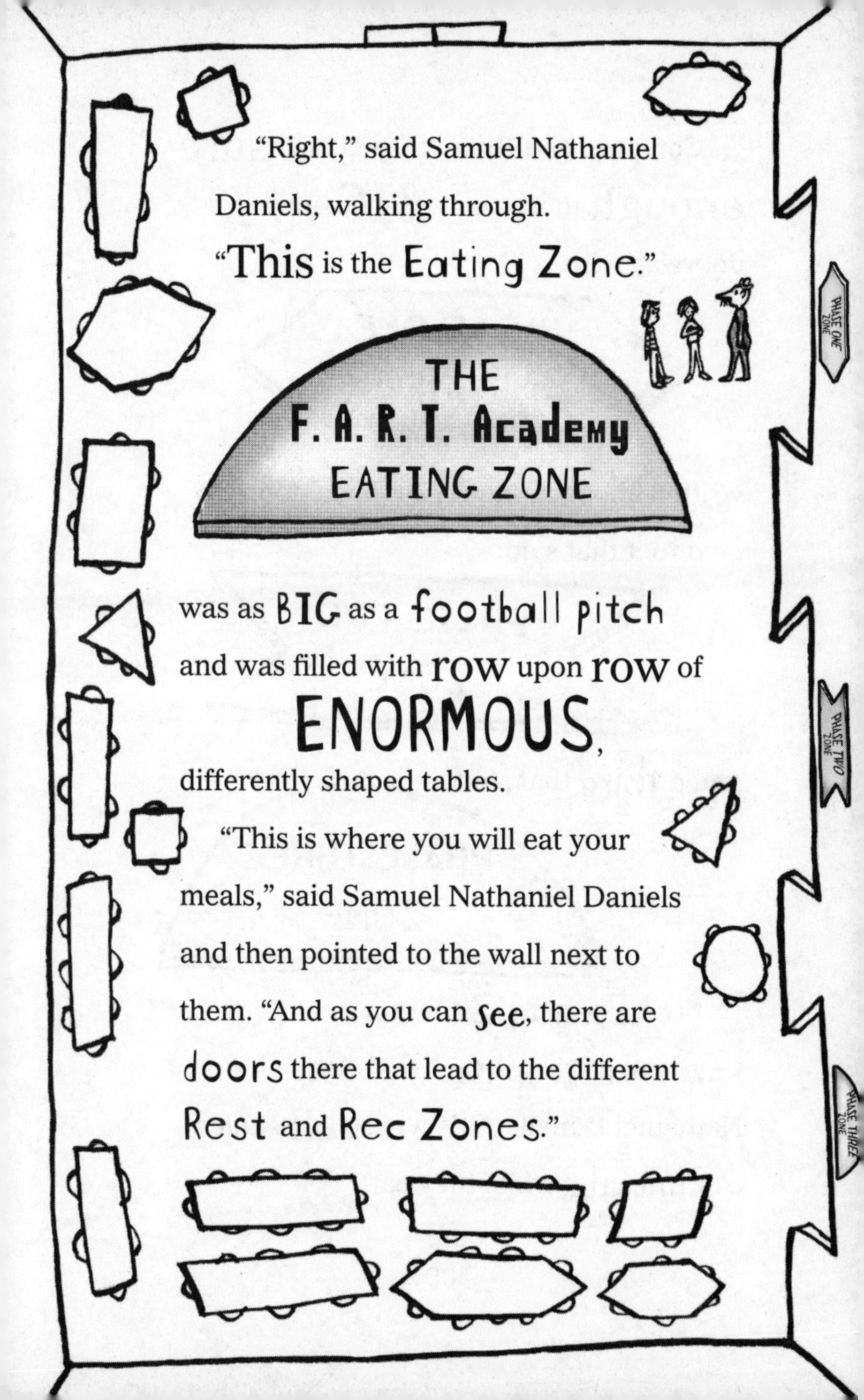

"Right," said Samuel Nathaniel Daniels, walking through. "This is the Eating Zone."

was as BIG as a football pitch and was filled with row upon row of ENORMOUS, differently shaped tables.

"This is where you will eat your meals," said Samuel Nathaniel Daniels and then pointed to the wall next to them. "And as you can see, there are doors there that lead to the different Rest and Rec Zones."

Compton and Bryan turned, and sure enough there was a BIG open doorway with

written above it, another open doorway next to it that said

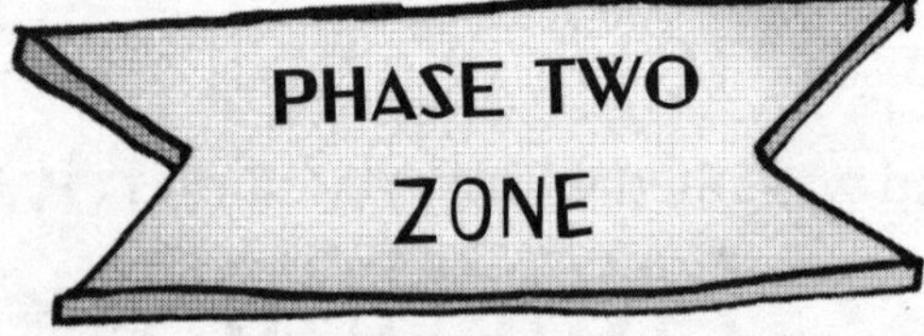

and a third that said

PHASE THREE ZONE.

"The Eating Zone is a communal space," said Samuel Nathaniel Daniels. "It's where all students can mingle while they eat."

"Where is everyone?" said Compton.

"We were the last to arrive so everyone else will be in their rooms," said Samuel Nathaniel Daniels, checking his **W.A.T.CH.** "Speaking of which, why don't we get you two into yours?"

Samuel Nathaniel Daniels led Compton and Bryan through the open doorway marked

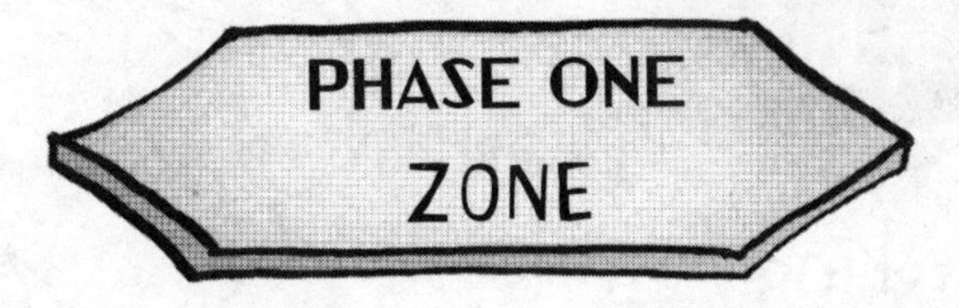

and into a room beyond. Well, I say "room" but it was so small that it was more like walking into a medium-sized shed.*

"Through there is the Rec Zone," said Samuel Nathaniel Daniels, gesturing to a door opposite them.

REC ZONE

* Except without the tools.**

** Or the lawnmower.***

*** Or the spiders.

"Feel free to use it anytime you're not otherwise occupied by your PHASE ONE TRAINING."

"What's *that?*" said Compton, pointing to a golden podium that stood in the middle of the tiny room.

Compton looked at Bryan suspiciously. He'd only had a few dealings with

BOGEY RECOGNITION TECHNOLOGY

and none of them had been at *all* pleasant.

"It's only just been installed and BOTH your snot patterns are in the system,"

said Samuel Nathaniel Daniels with a **big** smile on his face.

"ALL you have to do is get some bogeys on your hand, place it on the reader and it unlocks your own private room!"

Compton made a face and put his finger UP his nose.

"Not like *that*," said Samuel Nathaniel Daniels.

"As an added security measure, this computer needs a bit **more** of your hooter gunk to get a match. You need to have a good, **thick** layer of snot, so the best thing to do is blow your nose **into** your hand."

"*Seriously?*" said Compton.

"Seriously," nodded Samuel Nathaniel Daniels.

Compton looked at Bryan and rolled his eyes. He held his hand up to his nose, as if he had a hanky there, and

Great long ropes of snot...
...EXPLODED OUT
onto his hand...
...and glistened
like strings of pearls...
...under the BRIGHT LIGHTS of the tiny room.
Oooh, perfect,
said Samuel
Nathaniel Daniels.

"Right then, give it a good rub just to make sure the BRT can get a clear reading."

"The FPU couldn't use keys or fingerprints or anything like that?" muttered Compton to himself as he placed his snotty hand on the handprint-shaped reader, which immediately lit up red and flashed three times. Then a MECHANICAL VOICE said,

THANK YOU, ACADEMY AGENT VALANCE,

and a second later, three green lights appeared on the wall in front of them and a door, which up until that exact second had been completely INVISIBLE, s l o w l y hissed open to reveal a small flight of stairs.

"Excellent," said Samuel Nathaniel Daniels. "Your room is ready. Come on."

Chapter 8

IAN

At the top of the stairs, Compton couldn't quite believe what he saw.

said Samuel Nathaniel Daniels.

"B-b-but it's MASSIVE,"

said Compton, staggered that a room so large could be hiding on the other side of an invisible door that you opened up with a handful of snot.

Compton's bedroom was as dazzlingly white as the rest of the F. A. R. T. Academy and one wall was made entirely of GLASS.

Compton and Bryan walked across the room and stood gazing out of the ENORMOUS window as a hundred million pinpricks of LIGHT shimmered through the darkness from a city in front of them.

Where's THAT?

London?

said Bryan in amazement.

Well,

said Samuel Nathaniel Daniels.

It's actually what REPLACED London.

"*What?*" said Compton.

"Strictly speaking, though," added Samuel Nathaniel Daniels, "it's **what replaced** what *replaced* London."*

"Er, I see," said Bryan, who clearly **didn't**.

"So **where's** all my stuff?" asked Compton eagerly. "**Where** are the bed and the telly?"

"Sorry, I keep forgetting you're not from the twenty-seventh century," said Samuel Nathaniel Daniels, slapping his forehead. "Your room is **fully automated**, so if you want something, all you have to do is say it out loud and it APPEARS."

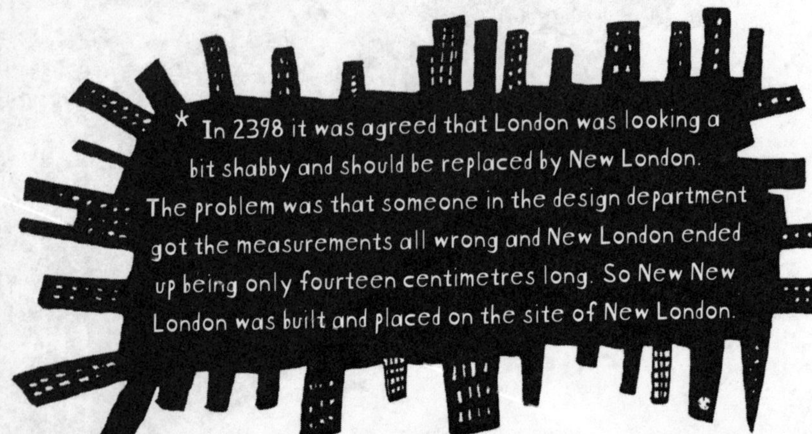

"So if I said '**wardrobe**'..." said Compton as a **wardrobe** **shot** out of the wall.

"Then it **APPEARS**," said Samuel Nathaniel Daniels, smiling.

"What if I **don't** want my **wardrobe** to appear?" said Compton as the **wardrobe**, on hearing the word "**wardrobe**" again, *slid* silently back into the wall.

Then don't say "wardrobe",

said Samuel Nathaniel Daniels as the wardrobe shot out of the wall again.

It's pretty simple really. EVERY time you say the thing you want, it APPEARS, and then EVERY time you say the thing AGAIN, it DISAPPEARS. WARDROBE!

Once again, the wardrobe slid silently back into the wall.

But WHAT if I want to say a sentence that has the word "wardrobe" in it,

said Compton, as the wardrobe shot out of the wall again.

BUT I don't want a wardrobe to shoot out of a wall?

The wardrobe slid silently back.

"Look," said Samuel Nathaniel Daniels a little peevishly, "why don't we just say that you will only say the word 'wardrobe'..." The wardrobe shot out of the wall "...when you want to use your wardrobe?" The wardrobe slid silently back into the wall.

"Otherwise," he continued, "there's no point in having an automated wardrobe!" The wardrobe shot out of the wall again.

Everyone was SILENT for a few moments before Samuel Nathaniel Daniels quietly said

Wardrobe

again and the wardrobe silently slid back into the wall.

Compton stared at Samuel Nathaniel Daniels.

"So what *other* **INCREDIBLE** technological wizardry do you have in the twenty-seventh century?" he asked, rolling his eyes.

"Let me show you how to operate what you call a **TV**," said Samuel Nathaniel Daniels. "**IAN**!"

Suddenly a man walked through the wall next to them into Compton's room. Compton's mouth dropped open.

he said, pointing at the man.

stammered Bryan.

"**Don't worry**, don't worry,"

laughed Samuel Nathaniel Daniels.

Samuel Nathaniel Daniels thought

for a moment.

Actually, to be more accurate,
IAN's MORE like a remote control
on a twenty-first century TV
and the BEST TV that anyone
has got in the WORLD
and an unbelievably AMAZING
games console
and the WHOLE of the internet.

gasped Bryan.

"Yup," said Samuel Nathaniel Daniels. "Well, apart from videos of cats. **IAN**'s got a bit of a **problem** with cats."

"So can we talk to him?" asked Compton.

"Of course," said Samuel Nathaniel Daniels. "He's here to help."

Er, **IAN**? said Compton.

Do you know who I am?

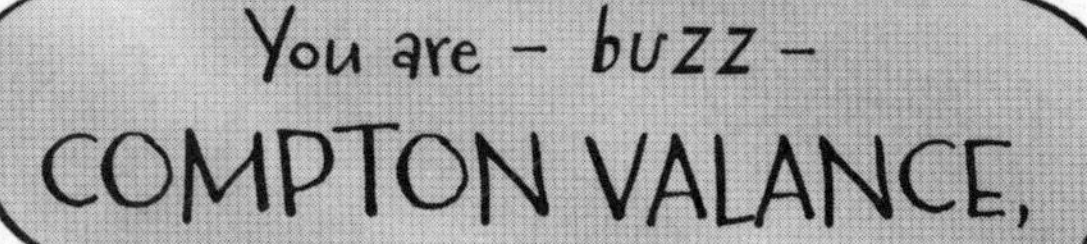

said **IAN** as he s l o w l y **flickered** and jerked.

You are – *buzz* – Academy Agent number 15.

shouted Compton.

said **IAN**.

Compton yawned a great big yawn.

"I think you need to get some sleep," said Samuel Nathaniel Daniels.

A LARGE and incredibly comfy-looking bed rose out of the floor.

"There you go," said Samuel Nathaniel Daniels. "Try it out for size."

"Mmmmmm," purred Compton as he climbed into the bed and pulled the covers over him. "Perfect. But I'm **not** going to sleep.

I want to see what else IAN can do."

"Alright," sighed Samuel Nathaniel Daniels. "But DON'T stay up all night. You've got a really important first day tomorrow."

"Where's my room?" said Bryan, yawning too.

"Oh, we just have to go back downstairs and put your snot onto the reader," said Samuel Nathaniel Daniels. "Then the BRT will find your bedroom door and make it APPEAR."

Bryan thought about saying something but then decided not to. It had been a

v e r y,

v e r y, v e r y

long day.

"Breakfast will be at 8.00 a.m. tomorrow morning," said Samuel Nathaniel Daniels as he and Bryan left Compton's room.

"Right, **IAN**," said Compton once Samuel Nathaniel Daniels and Bryan had gone. "Do you have a good game to play?"

IAN flickered for a moment.

"No," he said.

"*Oh,*" said Compton, a little disappointed.

I have seventeen million four hundred and twenty-five thousand one hundred and seventy GOOD games,

said **IAN**.

BRILLIANT, said Compton.

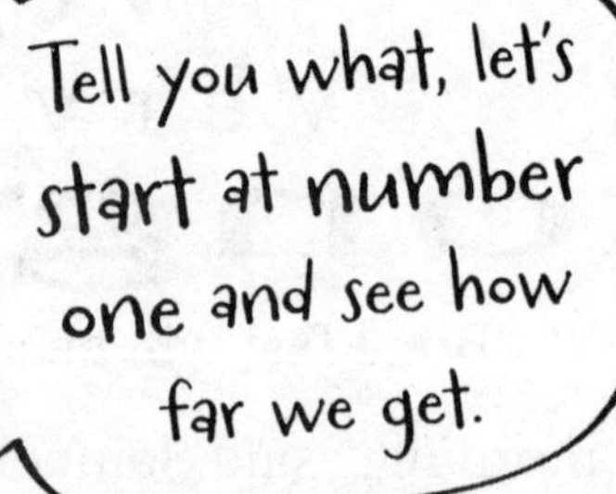

Chapter 9

The Return Of Silvermouth

Compton Valance?

Compton Valance?

COMPTONVALANCE
COMPTONVALANCE
COMPTONVALANCE!

Compton awoke with a start and sat **BOLT UPRIGHT** in his bed.

he **yelled** in confusion, still half asleep.

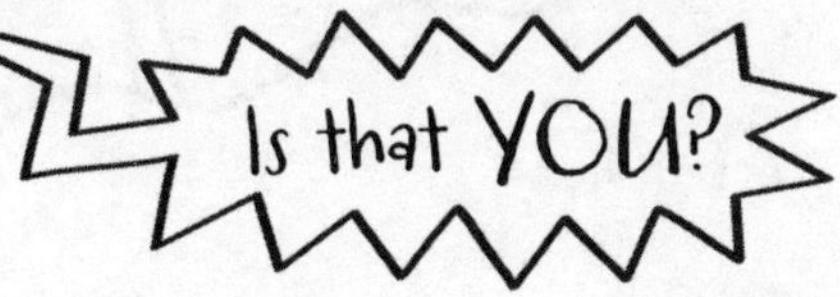

"Good morning – *buzz* – COMPTON VALANCE," said **IAN**, flickering by the side of Compton's bed.

Compton wiped the sleep from his eyes and ruffled his hair.

"Oh," he said, blinking and taking in his surroundings. "It's **you**, **IAN**. What do you *want?* What time is it?"

"This is your early morning wake-up alarm," said **IAN**. "It is now – *buzz* – 7.35 a.m. – *buzz*. Breakfast begins in the Eating Zone at 8.00 a.m. – *buzz*."

"What time did I get to sleep?" yawned Compton.

"Precisely – buzz – one hour and thirty-two minutes ago," said **IAN**. "Because of this I have prepared you a glass of SLUDGE."

A glass containing a **thick** brown liquid APPEARED from out of the wall beside Compton.

he said in disgust.

URGH, what's THAT?

"SLUDGE," repeated **IAN**. "It stands for Seriously Lovely Unbelievably Deliciously Gorgeous Elixir. It is a recipe I invented myself. I have given it to others who have had a late night and they found it – buzz – most invigorating."

Compton took the glass, *sniffed* the contents a couple of times, and then took the tiniest sip. A **funny thing** started to happen. Compton could feel his **whole body** sort of **tingle** and **quiver**. The **tingling** started off in his **toes** and then S l o w l y crept up his **legs**... then into his **tummy**... then down his **arms**... and then finally... into his **head**.

It was curious but where a few moments ago he felt

sleepy and snoozy

and other words that started with "S", now he felt suddenly all

zingy and ZIPPY

and other words that started with "Z".

"WOW, that's amazing," he said and drank the whole lot in one. "It's *sort of* like eating strawberries and fudge and electricity all at once. Right then, **IAN**, could you put some telly on, please?"

IAN flickered and was replaced by the HOLOGRAM of a newsreader sitting behind a desk emblazoned with the words

shouted the newsreader.**

* New (it was a new show) New New London News (about news in New New London... NOW! (news that was happening in New New London, right now).

** New New New London News... NOW!, replaced the old show that had been hosted by Drew and Suze called Drew's New New London News With Suze. It had been decided that Drew's New New New London News With Suze would have sounded silly so they gave the news show to Ted Stoat and gave Drew and Suze a new cookery, DIY, fashion, animal show with local traffic reports called Chews, Screws, Shoes, Zoos and Queues with Drew and Suze.

"Today's BIG NEWS STORY in New New London is the CAPTURE of the FPU's MOST WANTED time crim, **Gussage St Vincent.**"

While Ted Stoat talked about the news story, a HOLOGRAPHIC scene APPEARED beside him. It showed three people standing next to each other. Two of the people wore a strange black uniform that had the FPU logo on the front and helmets with silver visors that completely covered their faces. Compton barely noticed them because he couldn't take his eyes off the third figure, who was standing between the other two. He was a curiously dressed man who wore a long white wig, a red coat and a VAST moustache.

"In a DARING, early morning raid," continued Ted Stoat, "FPU Special Agents CAPTURED **St Vincent**, who will be taken to the FPU DETENTION ZONE and sent for trial at the next processing opportunity."

Compton watched as the HOLOGRAM of Gussage St Vincent flickered in the middle of his room. He saw a smile s l o w l y lick across St Vincent's face and two rows of sparkling, silver teeth glinted at him.

"You can put me in ANY PRISON you want," he said, tossing back the hair on his wig.

"NO PRISON CAN HOLD ME..." SINGS JAILBIRD GUSSAGE ST VINCENT

"Compton Valance – *buzz*," interrupted **IAN** flickering back into view. "Breakfast will begin in the Eating Zone in – *buzz* – four minutes. WARDROBE!"

Compton got out of bed, and narrowly avoided being SMASHED in the face as his wardrobe shot out of the wall and opened to reveal one bright red, tight onesie and one gold one.

"All **Academy Agents** – *buzz* – must wear the red uniform," said **IAN**. "Except on GRADUATION DAY when the ceremonial gold uniform is required."

Compton took the red uniform, pulled it on, then looked at it in the 3D mirror admiringly.*

* By the way, if you're currently yelling, "PANTS! PANTS! PANTS! FOR THE LOVE OF ALL THAT IS GOOD IN THE WORLD, WHY ISN'T HE WEARING ANY PANTS?" then there's a very simple explanation. By the twenty-seventh century, clothing design has evolved so much that breathable, lightweight, high-tech fabrics have rendered pants completely unnecessary. In fact, in the year 2664, you can wear your clothes for up to three months without having to get changed at all!

"Please take your InfoTab," said IAN, walking over and pointing to the bottom of the wardrobe. "You can use it for your work – *buzz*. There is also a **WELCOME BROCHURE** downloaded onto it, which explains everything that goes on here at the **F. A. R. T. Academy**."

Compton reached into the wardrobe and took out the InfoTab. "Cool," he said admiringly. "It's just like the one Samuel Nathaniel Daniels has."

"There is a – *buzz* – backpack too," continued IAN. "Please use it to carry your InfoTab."

Compton grabbed the backpack, put the InfoTab inside and slung it over his shoulder.

He couldn't wait to see Bryan and so he ran out of his room, and down the stairs as *FAST* as he **could**.

As he left his room he *knew* that

TODAY WAS GOING TO BE THE BEGINNING OF SOMETHING INCREDIBLE.

Chapter 10

Scawby Briggs

There was a **HUGE**, excited **HUBBUB** that greeted Compton as he walked into

The rows of different-shaped tables were full of students of ALL ages dressed in red uniforms and wearing **FPU** backpacks. Bryan was waiting for Compton by the **PHASE ONE** doorway.

"Did you stay up late?" he said excitedly. "What did you do with **IAN**?"

"Er, I played a game called

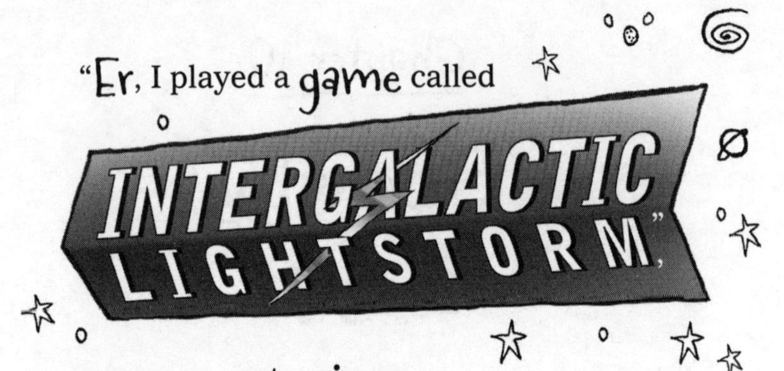

said Compton staring at an ENORMOUS bruise on Bryan's face. "How did you get that black eye?"

"Well, I spent most of the evening shouting out names of things and watching them pop out of walls," said Bryan. "Got caught out by the bin a couple of times. Have you seen where it comes from? Weird!"

There weren't many seats left but Compton spotted some space next to a girl and a boy who were sitting together at a table shaped like a large isosceles triangle.

"Quick, let's sit over there," he said to Bryan. "So where does the bin come from?"

As Bryan filled in Compton on the best way to dodge a surprising bin, a tall boy with dark hair who was sitting at a hexagon stuck his foot out right in Bryan's path.

Bryan tripped over the boy's foot and went CRASHING into a HEAP on the FLOOR.

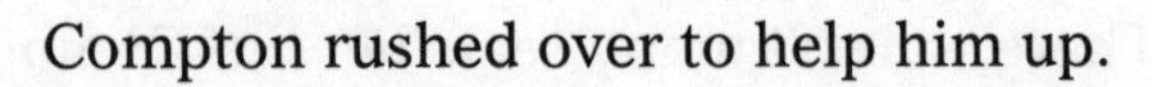

Compton rushed over to help him up. The dark-haired boy laughed **loudly** and *high-fived* the boy sitting next to him.

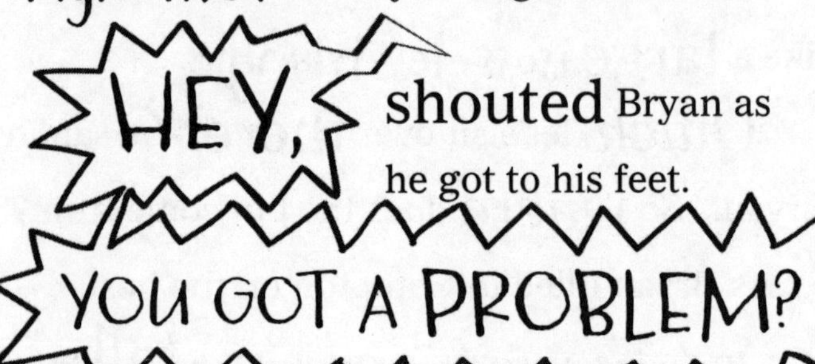

"HEY," **shouted** Bryan as he got to his feet. "YOU GOT A PROBLEM?"

The boy stood up from his chair *menacingly* and held Bryan's stare for a few seconds.

Then, letting out a 

he turned back to his friends, who **all** patted him on the back and laughed **very loudly**.

TEE HEE, HEE HEE...

"What's **his problem**?" said Compton as he and Bryan sat down at the triangle table.

"Don't worry about **Scawby**," said the girl sitting there. "He's a **TOTAL drongoid**."

"He's in **PHASE THREE** and tries to **BULLY everyone**," said the boy sitting with her. "He *thinks* he owns the place."

"That **knucklehead** sitting next to him is **Ulceby Goxhill**," said the girl. "They like to make **life** as **unpleasant** as possible for as **many people** as possible. By the way, I'm **Lola** and this is **Hector**."

"So are you guys **PHASE ONE** too?" said Hector. "You look kind of young."

"We're ten," said Compton.

"*Ten?*" spluttered Lola. "NO ONE *EVER* comes **here** aged *ten*."

"There **was** another ten year old," said Compton. "Mr Susan Glanville told us about him."

"*Mr Susan Glanville!*" said Hector in amazement. "THE *Mr Susan Glanville?* You've **met** him?"

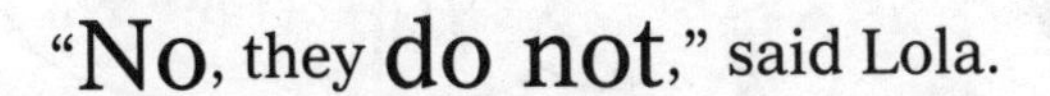

"No, they do not," said Lola. "Who *are* you, anyway?"

"Oh, I'm Compton," said Compton. "And this is Bryan."

Lola's jaw nearly hit the table.

"Compton Valance and Bryan Nylon," she said s l o w l y. "For real?"

Bryan and Compton looked at each other. Being recognized by people was really, *really* weird.

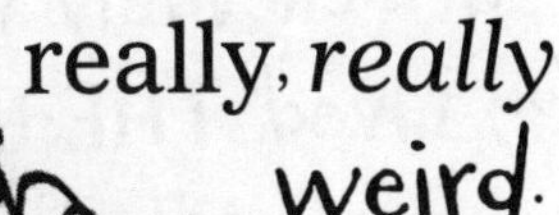

Yup 'fraid so,

said Compton, smiling.

Do you know us?

asked Bryan.

Are you *kidding?* said Hector, laughing.

EVERYBODY in the **world** knows who you two are. You're unbelievably famous. You saved **THE UNIVERSE** – it made ALL the news shows. There was a **song** about **you** that was number one for *five weeks!*

Number one? said Compton.

Five **weeks?** added Bryan.

Lola reached over and prodded Compton's arm, like she was checking to see if he was real.

"So you guys are from the twenty-first century," she said. "Incredible, what's it like?"

"Well, the home entertainment isn't quite as good as it is here," said Compton.

said Bryan, pulling his uniform out of his bum crack.*

* No pants took a bit of getting used to!

As they talked, a plate with three grey lumps materialized on the table in front of Compton. He looked around and saw that plates had APPEARED in front of the others too.

he said, eyeing the plate suspiciously.

"Oh, it's a perfect balance of all the vitamins and nutrients your body needs for the next five hours," said Lola, picking up a water pistol of clear liquid that appeared by her plate. "Just squirt the water over it and enjoy."

"Yum," whispered Bryan sarcastically. "Sounds delicious."

Compton and Bryan watched as Lola squeezed the water out of the water pistol and over the grey lumps on her plate. As soon as the water made contact, one grey lump turned brown, another turned dark green and the last turned an even darker shade of grey.*

* Food had changed quite a lot between the twenty-first and the twenty-seventh centuries. Delicious food was frowned upon as it did not provide a human body with any of the correct nutrition it required. Most twenty-seventh century humans ate grey food that tasted of damp rags.

Lola placed one of the lumps into her mouth and began to chew. It didn't look like she was enjoying it.

Compton nervously picked up his water pistol and squirted the water over his grey lumps, which, like Lola's, turned brown, green and darker grey. He picked the green one up and put a tiny piece in his mouth.

"It *sort* of tastes a bit like eating grass and dirt," he said, secretly wishing he had a glass of IAN's special SLUDGE.

"Yes," said Hector eagerly. "This batch is very grassy, isn't it? I'm also picking up a hint of damp leaf as well."

Bryan sniffed the grey lumps on his plate and picked up his water pistol.

"I could **murder** a sausage,"

he said as he began his very first

twenty-seventh century

breakfast. "*What's* for lunch? Baked

rabbit droppings?"

"No, it's soup, I *think*," said Lola.

As they finished their food, an "alarm"

sounded around the Eating Zone and

a MECHANICAL VOICE announced,

WOULD **ALL** ACADEMY AGENTS CHECK THEIR TIMETABLES AND MAKE THEIR WAY TO THEIR FIRST LESSON... PHASE ONE STUDENTS FOLLOW THE NAVIBOT... PHASE ONE STUDENTS FOLLOW THE NAVIBOT...*

* A NaviBot is a small robot whose only job is to show **PHASE ONE** students to their lessons. "Navi" stands for "navigation" and "bot" is short for "robot" and not for "bottom" as some people think. I mean, a bottom that can navigate would be really strange.

"What have we got first?" said Compton with a mouthful of brown lump.

Hector took an InfoTab out of his backpack and opened up the **PHASE ONE** timetable.

"Oh no!" he said. "It's UNDERSTANDING THE LAWS OF TIME. The teacher, Ms Drimpton, is supposed to be a

MONSTER."

"Ms Drimpton?" said Compton. "She *sounds* like an adorable silver-haired granny. Come on, *how* horrible can someone called Ms Drimpton *really* be?"

F. A. R. T. Academy

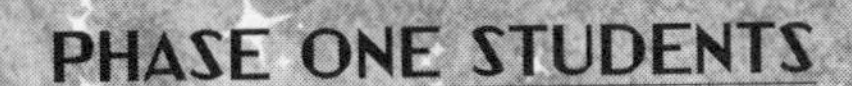

▼ *COURSE REQUIREMENTS*

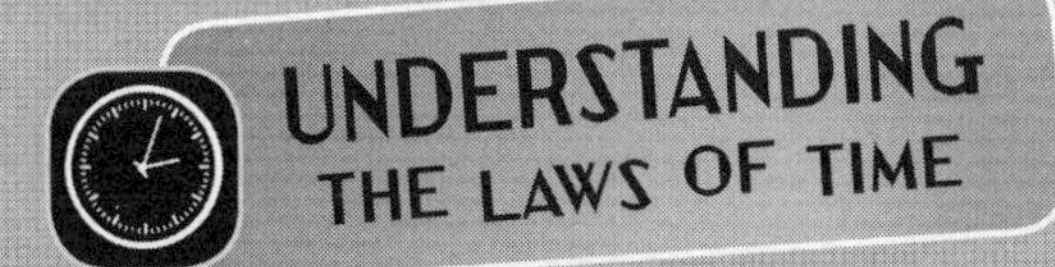

- By the end of the third month, students will be required to understand the fifty-eight separate Laws Of Time.
- Students will face a comprehensive sixteen-hour exam, one week before graduation.
- If you have any animal allergies, then please inform Student Services before attending class.

NOTE TO ALL STUDENTS

Soup of the day on Mondays is Formula 1.79*. Each portion comes with a flavour pouch** and an edible anti-bacterial lemon-scented towelette.

* In the twenty-seventh century, soup only comes in three flavours: tomato, vanilla and Formula 1.79, which looks a bit like frogspawn but doesn't actually taste of anything. You could if you wanted add some flavour with a flavour pouch.

** Flavour pouches come in two different flavours: tomato and vanilla.

Chapter 11

Q: How Horrible Can Someone Called Ms Drimpton *Really* Be?

A: VERY

WHAT are you snivelling LOT blabbering about?

snarled Ms Drimpton,

sitting at her desk at the front of her classroom.

Get a move on, you staggering bunch of drippy TWITS.

The excited chatter that had accompanied the PHASE ONE Academy Agents as they walked into the classroom died immediately. Compton, Bryan and the rest of the class quickly found their seats in absolute silence, just in case they got shouted at again.

Ms Drimpton was an extraordinary-looking woman. She wore large dark glasses, bright purple lipstick and her stone-grey hair was cut *so short* that her wrinkly, shrivelled face resembled a horrific, hundred-year-old peach that had had all the life and goodness SUCKED OUT of it by a witch.

"She looks like a bundle of fun," whispered Bryan as he and Compton sat down.

Perhaps even more surprising than Ms Drimpton's appearance was that of her tiny dog. It sat on the desk next to her. The dog (Compton wasn't sure if it was a boy dog or a girl dog*) was unlike ANY that Compton had seen before. It had a small body with a MASSIVE head and

ENORMOUS,

googly eyes

that bulged out of its skull as if attempting a daring escape. In its mouth were rows and rows of razor-sharp teeth, which were impossible to miss as the dog's gob constantly hung open, with its tongue unfurled and flapping in the breeze.

* Rather surprisingly, it was both.

"**Academy** Agents," snarled Ms Drimpton. "YOU have been invited to join the **Academy** and attempt PHASE ONE TRAINING because you have each demonstrated EXCEPTIONAL abilities that could be of use to the **FPU**. Or at least some of you have."

She paused again and Compton felt **certain** that she was looking over in his and Bryan's direction.

"This means NOTHING in my classroom," she snapped.

I don't care WHO you are and WHAT you've done to be here. You could have spent the last twenty years wiping the bottom of Queen Victoria's Sardinian pony for all I care. You could have travelled to the EDGE of

THE UNIVERSE

in a Roman chariot that you specially modified for the journey and had a delicious picnic while taking in the view.* I could NOT care LESS. You are ALL equally USELESS as far as I'm concerned.

* This would have been tricky for any of the 2664 Phase One Academy Agents to have done because modifying a Roman chariot wouldn't be accomplished for another 349 years, by a girl galled Pete from Tunbridge Wells.

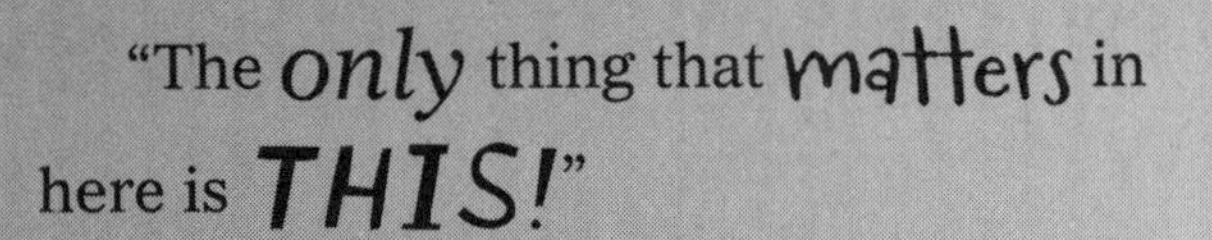

"The *only* thing that matters in here is **THIS!**"

Ms Drimpton pointed at a **HUGE** screen that materialized behind her. On the screen, the words

UNDERSTANDING THE LAWS OF TIME

APPEARED.

Her **MASSIVE**-headed dog growled menacingly.

GRR!

"*However,*" she continued, "**if** you study hard and **do *exactly*** as I say and **DON'T utter** a word unless I **specifically** ask you a **question**, and ***even then*** you answer the question **quickly** and then **SHUT** your **FAT GOB**, **THEN** you *might* just **stop** being a **HIDEOUS**, useless **worm** and **start** being a **HIDEOUS**, slightly-less-useless **worm**."

Compton couldn't be sure but he thought the dog sniggered at this.

he whispered to Bryan.

"YOU!" yelled Ms Drimpton and pointed at Compton. "STAND UP. WHAT'S YOUR NAME?"

Compton's face felt HOT as he stood up. Ms Drimpton's dog barked twice.

"Er, Compton," he said, his voice quivering.

Oh yessssssssssssss,

sneered Ms Drimpton as she stood up from her desk and stalked over to where Compton was standing.

The WORLD FAMOUS Mr Compton Valance.

A gasp went around the room as people started whispering Compton's name.

screeched Ms Drimpton to the class, and then turned around to face Compton, who shuffled awkwardly on his feet. "I forgot to say that there is another thing that I DON'T care for," she said, so menacingly that each wrinkle on her face quivered. "And THAT is a child who *thinks* they are better than the rest of us."

Compton opened his mouth to speak but couldn't get a word in as the Drimpton onslaught continued.

"You may **THINK** you are *famous* and *la-de-da* just because you '**SAVED THE UNIVERSE**'," *spat* Ms Drimpton, "but you are **no more** *special* than **anyone** else."

"*B-but*," stammered Compton. "I *don't* think I'm more—"

screamed Ms Drimpton so *shrilly* that her dark glasses nearly fell off her face.

said Compton.

"I said SILENCE!" shrieked Ms Drimpton. "Go and sit on your own in the corner and wear the Fruity Hat Of Shame for the rest of the lesson."

Compton's face went red again and burned at the injustice of what was happening.

"And if you continue to question my authority," snapped Ms Drimpton, "I will report you to Mr Susan Glanville. Now MOVE!"

The room was deadly quiet as Compton walked from his desk to the tiny one in the corner and put on a large TOP HAT covered in exotic fruits.*

* No one was really very sure why Ms Drimpton made people wear the Fruity Hat Of Shame. Some said that it was because when she was younger she'd been tricked by an apricot and had developed a deep mistrust of fruit ever since.

"Right," said Ms Drimpton. "Let's get on with the lesson, *shall we?* UNDERSTANDING THE LAWS OF TIME. The FIRST LAW OF TIME was created in 2509 blah blah blah blahdy blahdy blah blah..."

Compton watched as his classmates tapped away on their InfoTabs. He groaned silently to himself and a grape fell off the hat and BOPPED him on the nose. This was definitely not what he thought becoming a time-travely agenty thingy in the twenty-seventh century would be like at all.

Chapter 12

A Very Fortunate Call

After a draining morning with Ms Drimpton, Compton and Bryan had some vanilla soup followed by an edible, anti-bacterial, lemon-scented towelette in the Eating Zone, and then an afternoon of

USEFUL TIME-TRAVEL LANGUAGES:

ANCIENT GREEK, EGYPTIAN AND MICROWAVE.*

* It was important for all Academy Agents to have a basic understanding of all the major languages spoken through the history of civilization. The pings of a microwave were used as the major world language during a brief but important two-week period in the twenty-fourth century.

At the end of a long first day, they walked back to the PHASE ONE Rec Zone with their new friends Lola and Hector.

"Anyone fancy a game of SUPERFIVES?" asked Lola.

"What's SUPERFIVES?" said Bryan.

"Er, only the greatest sport in the HISTORY OF THE WORLD," she replied. "You must have heard of it."

Compton and Bryan shook their heads.

"Nope," said Compton.

"Is it like snooker?" said Bryan. "I'm quite good at that."

Lola shook her head.

"Nah," she laughed. "It's much better than snooker. Come on, I'll show you."*

* Surprisingly, of all the games played in the twenty-first century, only snooker and darts were still played in the twenty-seventh century.

They walked through the **PHASE ONE** doorway and into the Rec Zone. Despite being almost E M P T Y, it was clear something was very, very

WRONG.

On the other side of the room they could see one of their classmates, a girl called Lotty Clare, in tears while Scawby Briggs shouted,

LOTTY CLARE, BOTTY HAIR.
LOTTY CLARE, BOTTY HAIR,

at her. Ulceby Goxhill stood next to him, laughing, as Scawby taunted Lotty, grabbed her glasses from her face and **PUSHED** her to the floor.

shouted Scawby cruelly as he put on Lotty's glasses and pranced around the room.

"Huh huh huh," grunted Ulceby Goxhill, like an ape that had just had its brain removed and replaced by a plate of trifle.

"HEY!" Compton yelled and dashed over to help.

He ran **straight** into Scawby and shoved him **hard** in the chest...

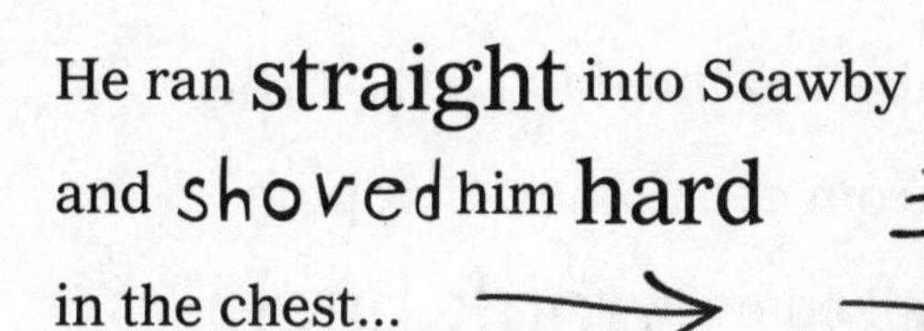

...Scawby **hadn't** seen Compton coming and was thrown off balance by the shove...

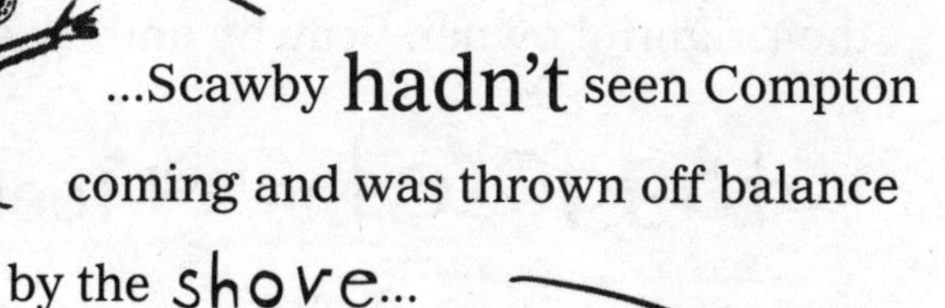

...He fell backwards onto the floor and landed with a crash over by a **Super*fives*** pod.

Ulceby Goxhill was just *about* to attack Compton when Bryan *rushed* in and **rammed** him as **hard** as he could too...

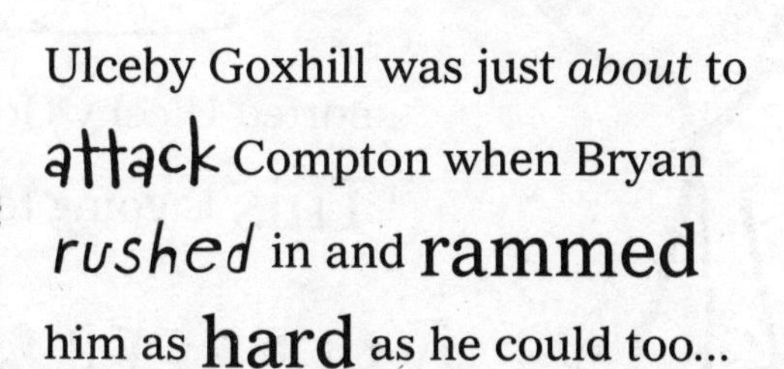

...Goxhill landed in a **HEAP** on top of Scawby Briggs.

As the pair attempted to untangle themselves from each other, Compton calmly walked over, took back Lotty's glasses and returned them to their rightful owner. Scawby and Ulceby staggered to their feet in a most undignified way.

"You two are going to regret that," Scawby said with a snarl.

Huh huh huh,

snorted Ulceby Goxhill. "This is going to be fun."

BLEEP BEEP

BLEEP BEEP

BLEEP BEEP

"Oh, *man*," said Scawby Briggs as his clenched fist started to ring. "Looks like we'll have to continue this another time, *Valance*."

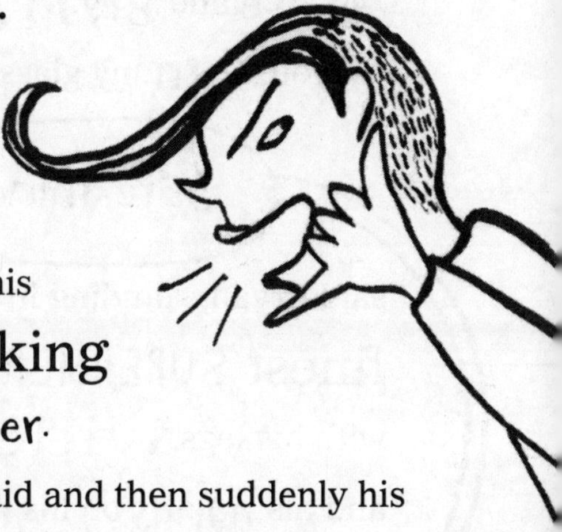

He glared at Compton for a moment and then put his thumb in his ear and started talking into his little finger.

"*What?*" he said and then suddenly his voice lowered. "D-did everything go *okay*?"

Too engrossed in his call to care about Compton any more, Scawby Briggs left the PHASE ONE Rec Zone.

Ulceby Goxhill followed him but deliberately barged into Compton as he left.

"Are you alright, Lotty?" asked Bryan, rushing over.

"Yeah, I think so," she said. "Thanks, guys. That was pretty AWESOME. I can't believe I was just saved by Compton Valance and Bryan Nylon. Will you sign my glasses case?"

Sure thing,

said Bryan, standing in his finest SUPERHERO stance with his legs **wide** apart and his hands on his hips,

I don't think that'll be the LAST we see of him, though. Not by a long way.

Bryan's track record at "getting things right" was not very good at all. When he was four he had thought that you could wash your hands by weeing on them.*
When he was six he had put a spider in his mouth to see "if it tasted like chicken".**

And in one of their first TIME TRAVEL TRIPS he had caused the early extinction of the dinosaurs by letting them eat a packet of custard creams.
Rather unfortunately for Compton though, Bryan was right about this. It was definitely *not* the LAST they'd see of Scawby Briggs.

* You can't!
** It didn't!***
*** I wouldn't advise trying either of the above. EVER.

F. A. R. T. Academy

★ WELCOME BROCHURE ★

▼ SUPER*FIVES*

- For those who have never played **SUPER*FIVES*** before, you are in for a treat.

- It was devised by Lester Shear in the year 2455 as a way for brain surgeons to relax during operations.

- **SUPER*FIVES*** was originally played on any old KlubbBall court using a Class Three Hoverboard and five practice Klubbs.

- It took off in popularity immediately and children started playing it in the streets, marking out a **SUPER*FIVES*** course with laserchalk.

- In the twenty-seventh century, the game is played on both human worlds and has become the favourite global sport of Earth 1.*

* Another human world was needed in the year 2388 after a particularly heated game of tiddlywinks got a bit out of hand. Let's just say there were faults on both sides and leave it at that!

HOW TO PLAY

- **SUPER*FIVES*** is played in a small pod, about the size of a Size Ten Charging Unit (this was a deliberate design feature so that a pod could fit into any home or office space).

- Once you step inside the **SUPER*FIVES*** pod, the interior expands to an infinite size and shape. Then, in a randomly chosen, computer-generated landscape, a player uses a hoverboard to fly around and attempts to shoot five small balls at five small targets.

For Earth 1 **SUPER*FIVES*** rules, TAP HERE

For Earth 2 **SUPER*FIVES*** rules, TAP HERE

Chapter 13

A Few Moments *Before* The End Of Chapter 12

In a dark, dank room, a man with a golden earring sat at a desk. Using only the flickering light coming from the corridor outside, he dialled a number on the palm of his hand and put his thumb into his ear.

CLICK

They GOT him yesterday and took him in,

he said into his little finger.

Aaarrr, it DIDN'T go quite as we'd planned.

The man listened and grunted.

But, we ARE chartin' a course for smoother waters, lad. The plan is back on track so YOU needs to be ready for action,

he said in a deep, rasping voice.

When he's out, we WON'T have long. I'll be in touch.

And with that the man with the golden earring pushed a button and the line CLICKED off. He rubbed his stubbly chin and laughed a low and horrible laugh.

HA HA HA HA
HAAAAARRRRRRR!!
AAARRRRRR...

Chapter 13A

F.A.R.T. Academy

★ WELCOME BROCHURE ★

PHASE ONE STUDENTS

▼ ***WEEKLY TIMETABLE***

MONDAY *MORNING*

Lesson: Understanding the Laws of Time
Teacher: Ms Drimpton
Special notes: Do not look dog directly in eye!
Do not bring up the subject of fruit!

MONDAY *AFTERNOON*

Lesson: Useful Time Travel Languages:
Ancient Greek, Egyptian and Microwave
Teacher: Mr Spencer

TUESDAY *MORNING*

Lesson: Time Machine Maintenance
Teachers: Mrs Herberts and Ms George
Special notes: Please remember to bring F.A.R.T. Academy approved welding mask. This year, swimming goggles will not be allowed as a suitable alternative!

TUESDAY *AFTERNOON*

Lesson: Twenty-seventh Century Citizen Studies
Teacher: Mr Bruanski
Special notes: This term Mr Bruanski wishes to show you what being a citizen was like in the fourteenth century. Please make sure your bubonic plague jabs are up-to-date. If in doubt make an appointment at the MediZone.

WEDNESDAY *MORNING*

Lesson: Time Portals: Rips, Tunnels and Punctures
Teacher: Mr Milton Abbas (robot)
Special notes: Due to an unfortunate situation in last year's class, where a lesson about Time Tunnels got out of hand, Mr Milton Abbas will this year be replaced by a robot bearing the same name.

WEDNESDAY *AFTERNOON*

Lesson: Time Mapping
Teacher: Mr Chowdry and Mr Chowdry
Special notes: As they are identical twins, Mr Chowdry will always wear scarlet-coloured shoes whereas Mr Chowdry's shoes will be plain red (for ease of identification).

THURSDAY *MORNING*

Lesson: Historic Time Machines
Teacher: Mr Ryan Bobson
Special notes: In case of a flare-up of one of Mr Bobson's allergies, please make your way to the Time Museum.

THURSDAY *AFTERNOON*

Lesson: Homework Session
Teacher: Dr Bongo
Special notes: As usual, please submit all special homework queries to Dr Bongo by Tuesday morning at the latest. He will require at least fifty hours notice for any time-travel permits and/or use of **FPU** equipment.

FRIDAY *MORNING*

Lesson: **SUPER*FIVES*** Practice
Teacher: Mrs Peter Llanelli
Special notes: Please remember your shoes.

FRIDAY *AFTERNOON*

Lesson: Time Crime: A History of
Teacher: Special Agent 12

Chapter 14

Just Over Two Weeks Later...

Compton Valance?

Compton Valance?

COMPTONVALANCE
COMPTONVALANCE
COMPTONVALANCE!

Compton jumped up in his bed.

What? What?
WHAT?

he said,

blinking

his bleary eyes.

"Good morning – buzz – Compton Valance,"

said IAN as the blinds across the window

slowly melted away, allowing

the sunlight to stream in the room.

"I have got to change your alarm settings,"

said Compton, breathing a big sigh of relief

and reaching for the glass of SLUDGE

that APPEARED from the wall beside him.

"Today is – buzz – Friday," said IAN calmly.

And with **that IAN**

DISAPPEARED.

Ted Stoat from the

show **flickered** to life.

Hi, I'm TED STOAT,

said the HOLOGRAM

of Ted Stoat.

"Er, I know!" said Compton to the HOLOGRAM, which obviously couldn't hear him or respond.

Once AGAIN, Stoat continued, the NEWS this morning is ALL about the WORLD'S MOST NOTORIOUS time crim, **Gussage St Vincent.**

"I wonder what he did to become so notorious," said Compton to himself as he pulled on his **F. A. R. T. Academy** uniform and admired himself in the 3D mirror.

There were DRAMATIC SCENES this morning when Judge Julie SENTENCED **St Vincent** to ONE THOUSAND YEARS IN PRISON for his time crimes. Let's now go LIVE to the courthouse and speak to our reporter Lenny Cubbage, who's RIGHT THERE on the scene.

The picture cut to a shot of a bald man in an overcoat standing outside a grand-looking building.

"Thanks, Ted," said Lenny Cubbage.

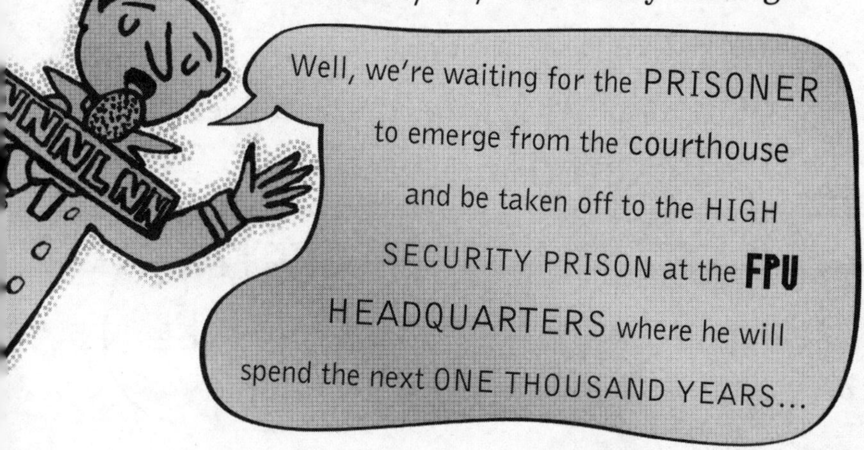

Well, we're waiting for the PRISONER to emerge from the courthouse and be taken off to the HIGH SECURITY PRISON at the FPU HEADQUARTERS where he will spend the next ONE THOUSAND YEARS...

As Lenny Cubbage delivered his report, the doors of the courthouse behind him opened and out came a tall man wearing a wig, a red jacket and sporting a COLOSSAL moustache. His hands were tied together with some sort of laser chain and he was led by a group of **FPU Special Agents** wearing black helmets with silver visors.

"And THERE'S **Gussage St Vincent** now," said Lenny Cubbage as he raced up the steps of the courthouse and thrust his microphone underneath the nose of St Vincent. "Do you have ANYTHING to say about your SENTENCE?"

Gussage St Vincent's black eyes **flickered** like a lizard's.

he said with a smirk on his face that showed off two rows of GLEAMING silver teeth.

It was strange but Compton had the feeling that Gussage St Vincent was looking **straight** at **him**.

"However," he continued, "the time I *do* spend in this PRISON will be spent thinking about COMPTON VALANCE."

Before he could say anything else, he was bundled away by the **FPU Special Agents**.

yelled Compton and the sneering HOLOGRAPHIC face of Gussage St Vincent froze before him. Suddenly, **IAN flickered** back in the room.

"Compton Valance," he said. "It is now – *buzz* – 8.25 a.m. The **NaviBot** is waiting downstairs in the Eating Zone. Please leave *immediately*."

But Compton wasn't listening and it DIDN'T matter anyway because a moment later the air in Compton's room crackled and fizzed and Samuel Nathaniel Daniels

APPEARED.

Compton,

he said in a **very**, *very* serious voice.

I need YOU to come with us to the FPU HQ. We'll pick Bryan up on the way. The Commissioner has to see you two, RIGHT NOW.

Chapter 15

An URGENT Meeting In A Secret Room

Ten minutes later, in a secret room hidden behind a door in the **FPU** HQ marked

WOMEN'S TOILETS

The Commissioner, Samuel Nathaniel Daniels and Mr Susan Glanville all stood looking at Compton and Bryan.

"I guess this is about the news report," whispered Bryan.

Compton nodded.

"It goes without saying," said The Commissioner, "that we are taking this incident very, *very* seriously. Gussage St Vincent will be held in the special **FPU Time Crim prison**. It is the highest security unit EVER created."

said Bryan suspiciously.

"Well," said The Commissioner, "Gussage will spend the next one thousand years in a steel-lined prison cell with laser bars covering the walls, roof and floor."

"Wow," said Bryan, clearly impressed. "That's pretty high."

"That's not all," continued The Commissioner. "His cell is surrounded by a moat filled with lava and lava-resistant electric eels."

"*Wow!*" said Bryan again. "That's much **higher**."

"That's **not** all," continued The Commissioner. "The moat is, in turn, surrounded by *another* lava moat."

"WOW!" said Bryan again. "That's *even* **higher!**"

"That's **not** all," continued The Commissioner. "The lava-filled moat that surrounds the *other* lava-filled moat, is in turn surrounded by *another* lava-filled moat."

"WOW!" said Bryan again. "That's unbelievably **high**!"

"That's **not** all," continued The Commissioner. "We have buried his cell and the three moats four hundred metres **below** ground level."

"WOW!" said Bryan again.

"That *must* be as **high** as you can go!"

"**And,**" said The Commissioner, "his cell has been placed in a Dungeon of Infinity for an indefinite period."

Bryan was about to say "wow" again but decided not to, as he didn't have the foggiest notion what a Dungeon of Infinity actually **was**.

"However, just to put your mind at rest," said The Commissioner, "I have **also** put extra security guards on alert within the **FPU** and the **F. A. R. T. Academy**."

Compton stood there in *total* **silence**.

"You okay?" said Bryan.

WHY me?

Compton said eventually.

WHY did Gussage St Vincent say MY name?

"We're not sure yet," said The Commissioner kindly. "But we do know that when we went inside his secret hideout yesterday, we found your FPU file."

"It had been stolen from my office a few weeks ago," said Samuel Nathaniel Daniels.

"Why didn't you tell me my file had been stolen?" said Compton.

Samuel Nathaniel Daniels looked a bit embarrassed and mouthed the word "sorry" to Compton.

"So, what has he done?" said Compton eventually. "Why is Gussage St Vincent so DANGEROUS?"

The Commissioner looked at Mr Susan Glanville who sighed a big sigh.

Chapter 16

THE GIGANTUS MACHINE

Mr Susan Glanville took a long drink from his cup and put it down on The Commissioner's desk. Compton and Bryan, both sitting now, watched as he prowled around the room.

This ALL goes back over thirty years to the year 2632,

Mr Susan Glanville began.

"Gussage St Vincent?"

said Bryan eagerly.

Mr Susan Glanville nodded.

he said.

"He spent all his spare time during PHASE ONE TRAINING working on a secret project in one of the test laboratories and on the night before the big graduation ceremony, he invited me to come and see what it was."

Mr Susan Glanville took another long drink. Compton could see that his hands were trembling.

"His secret project," he continued, "was to create his own TIME MACHINE – one so POWERFUL that it could

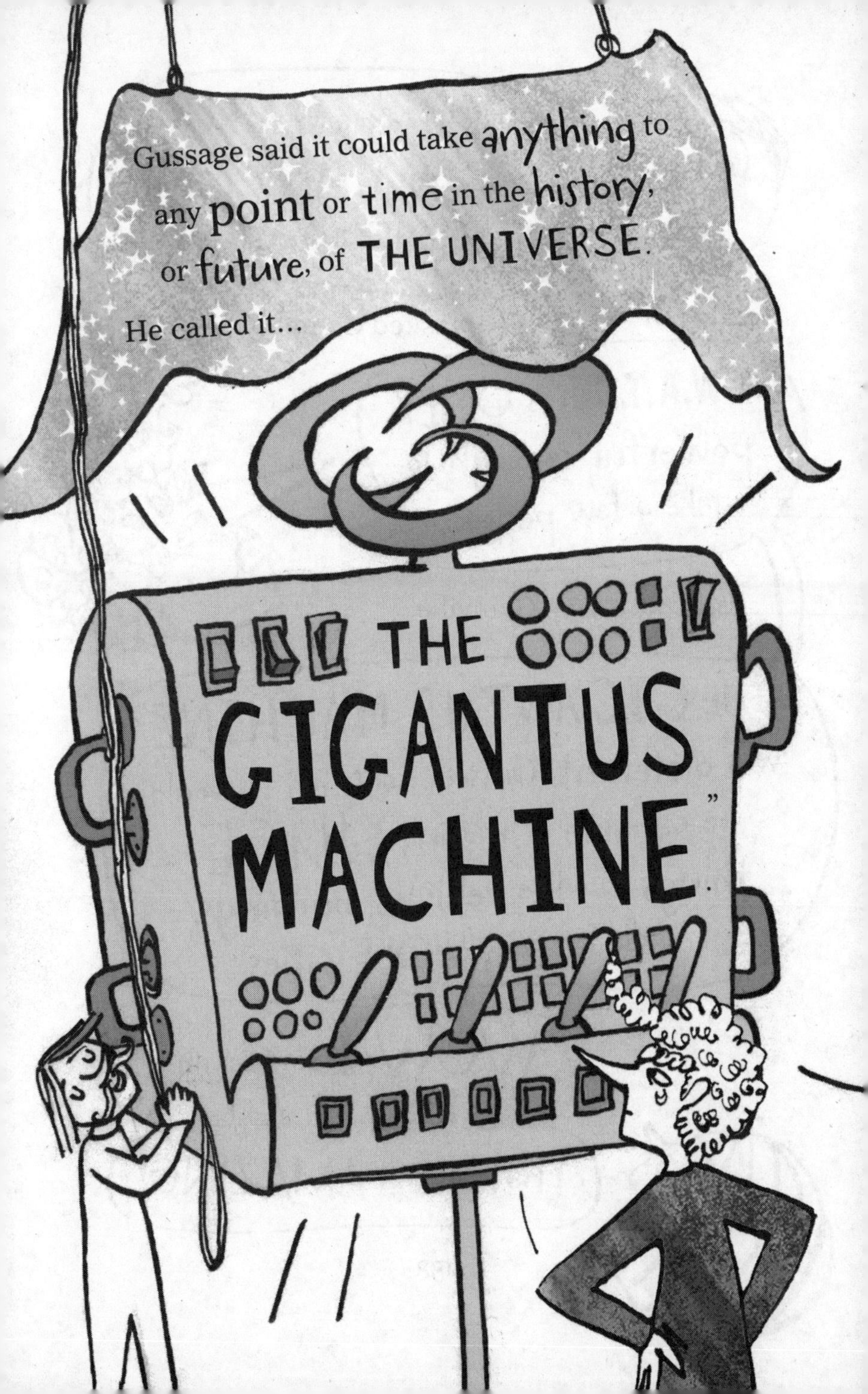
Gussage said it could take anything to any point or time in the history, or future, of THE UNIVERSE.
He called it...
"THE GIGANTUS MACHINE".

But can't a **W.A.T.CH.** take you to ANY point in TIME and SPACE?

asked Compton.

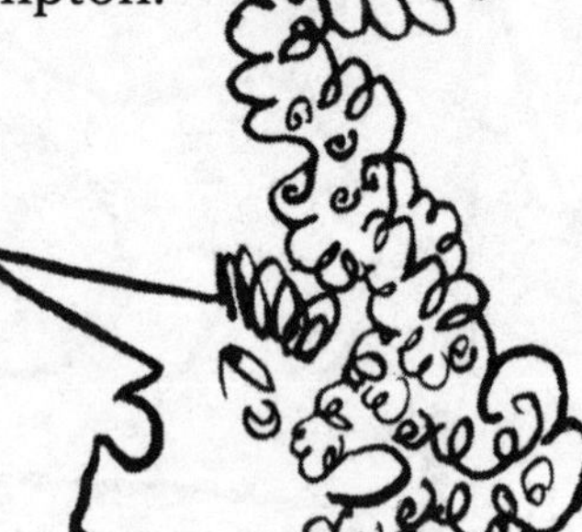

A **W.A.T.CH.** is ONLY powerful enough to take a few people,

said Mr Susan Glanville.

THE GIGANTUS MACHINE was different. Gussage said that it would be capable of moving HUGE things too, like vehicles, buildings, maybe even WHOLE cities.

WOW, said Bryan.

That sounds AMAZING!

In some ways, said Mr Susan Glanville.

BUT it was also very, very DANGEROUS. This was something that Gussage was too young to fully understand. Imagine the DAMAGE that a machine as POWERFUL as THE GIGANTUS MACHINE could have done. As soon as I saw it I KNEW that if it got into the wrong hands it would mean the

END OF LIFE

AS WE KNEW IT.

"So what *happened?*" said Bryan.

"As it turned out, he'd put a couple of wires in the wrong way round so it didn't work properly," said Mr Susan Glanville.

"In fact, as soon as he turned the MACHINE on, it became pretty obvious that things were not going to plan."

"How could you tell?" asked Bryan.

"Well," said Mr Susan Glanville.

"I first had the tiniest suspicion when THE GIGANTUS MACHINE

"Woah," said Bryan.
A piece of the MACHINE flew through the air and HIT ME in the face, giving me THIS scar,
said Mr Susan Glanville, rubbing his cheek.
"So what happened to Gussage St Vincent?"
said Compton.

"We *thought* that Gussage had simply, but rather tragically, BLOWN himself to smithereens," said The Commissioner, opening a drawer in her desk. "And then two years ago, we received **this letter** from him."

She handed Compton an old, tattered and scorched piece of paper.

Looking at it he could just make out a faded message in inky handwriting.

Gussage St Vincent,
June 23rd, 1731.
15°50'N 61°36'W

1731?

said Compton.

"When THE GIGANTUS MACHINE EXPLODED," explained The Commissioner, "it created a momentary TIME PORTAL that sucked St Vincent from the twenty-seventh century and BACK IN TIME to the early 1700s.

We obviously had NO IDEA that this had happened. Those numbers at the end of the message are co-ordinates. He *knew* that once **we** had them, we'd be able to go BACK IN TIME and pick him up."

Compton looked at the writing.

"The co-ordinates and date led us to a small, uninhabited Caribbean island," said Samuel Nathaniel Daniels. "We found Gussage all alone and he told us he'd been dumped there by a group of dastardly pirates."

"*Pirates?*" said Bryan.

"So we brought him back here but the next day he VANISHED", said Samuel Nathaniel Daniels. "You see, whilst it was true that he had been taken to the small, uninhabited island by a group of dastardly

pirates, what he didn't tell us was that HE was the leader of the group of dastardly pirates and had ordered them to take him to the small, uninhabited island."

"What? I DON'T understand." said Compton.

"THE GIGANTUS MACHINE had sent him back to the year 1702," said Samuel Nathaniel Daniels. "He woke up on a pirate ship called *Fandango's Revenge*. He would have been thrown overboard if he hadn't persuaded them to keep him as a cabin boy."

said Bryan.

Well, at first he was too busy trying to stay alive,

said Samuel Nathaniel Daniels.

And besides, have you EVER tried to post a letter on-board a pirate ship?

Er, NO, said Bryan.

Well, said Samuel Nathaniel Daniels, it's very, very TRICKY.

said Compton.

He became a cabin boy on the ship,

said Samuel Nathaniel Daniels.

The only problem was that he LOVED being a pirate! He LOVED the excitement, the adventure, the looting, the stealing, the treasure, the clothes, EVERYTHING. When he was twenty-one he THREW the captain of *Fandango's Revenge* overboard and took FULL COMMAND of the ship.

At some point he got his teeth replaced with silver ones and renamed his pirate crew The Fearless.

That's INCREDIBLE! said Compton.

After that he spent the next few years stealing and plundering and burying treasure,

continued Samuel Nathaniel Daniels.

He did marry a woman called Bertha in 1724 and started a family but eventually got bored, stole ALL her jewels and went back to his ship and crew.

"The Fearless stole more **gold** and **jewels** than ANY pirates had EVER done before."*

"So *if* he **loved** it so much, then *why* did he come back?" said Compton.

"We'd like to know that too," said The Commissioner. "The day after he got back, he told us his version of what had happened over the last thirty years—"

"Told you a **complete load** of old garbage, you mean?" said Bryan.

"Well, *quite*," said the Commissioner. "Then he stole a **W.A.T.CH.** and DISAPPEARED. Er, **again**."

* The FPU found out about the real Gussage St Vincent when they realized the famous sea shanty "The Silver Toothed Man" was all about his lowdown, dirty deeds.

"He's a devious and dishonest snake, only thinks 'bout the loot he will take, with a yo-ho-ho, ho-ho-ho, yo, beware the silver-toothed man.
He came fizzin' and cracklin' to life, so wicked he stole from his wife, with a yo-ho-ho, ho-ho-ho, yo, beware the silver-toothed man..."

"That was two years ago," said Mr Susan Glanville. "And since then he has stolen a whole load of FPU equipment and gone on at *least* seven unauthorized TIME-TRAVEL trips."

"So he must have come back because he wanted something," said Compton. "But *what?*"

"It's got to have something to do with YOU," said Bryan. "Otherwise *why* did he mention *your* name?"

"DON'T let your imagination run away with you," said The Commissioner. "We don't know what he's up to at the moment."

"I *know*," said Compton nervously. "That's exactly what I'm afraid of."

Chapter 17

An EXCITING Announcement

When Compton and Bryan returned to the F. A. R. T. Academy, things were unusually quiet. The other PHASE ONE students were in the SUPERFIVES pods, and everyone else was in classes.

In fact, the only NOISE that broke the quiet was a familiar voice booming all around the Eating Zone. Compton looked to see where it was coming from and there, projected high onto the wall, was the

GIANT

HOLOGRAPHIC HEAD

of Mr Susan Glanville.

The HOLOGRAM was clearly a recording as he repeated the same message three times.

HELLO, STUDENTS!

he bellowed.

I HAVE AN EXCITING ANNOUNCEMENT FOR YOU. THIS YEAR'S GRADUATION DAY WILL BE *EVEN BETTER* THAN USUAL. A WONDERFUL NEW EXHIBIT WILL BE UNVEILED AFTER THIS YEAR'S GRADUATION CEREMONY. MORE DETAILS COMING SOON. SEE YOU THERE. 3.45 P.M. ON THE 22ND AUGUST!

After it had repeated the same message three times, the HOLOGRAM DISAPPEARED. Compton turned to Bryan.

"*Talking posters?*" he said. "That is really COOL!"

"Fancy trying a game of **SUPER*FIVES***?" said Bryan. "Some of the pods should be free."

"Great idea," said Compton excitedly, but as they tried to go through the PHASE ONE ZONE doorway, they found their path BLOCKED by Scawby Briggs and Ulceby Goxhill.

"Going somewhere?" said Briggs as he PUSHED Compton back with a little shove.

"We... We..." said Bryan.

"Wee wee? You're going for a *wee-wee?*" laughed Briggs, grabbing a handful of Bryan's hair and pulling it **hard**.

Then he shoved Bryan so *hard* that he fell backwards onto the floor. Ulceby Goxhill snorted like a BADGER with a sinus problem.

"Leave him ALONE," said Compton, helping his friend to his feet.

"Or *what?*" snapped Briggs. "You better watch yourself, Valance, and do you want to KNOW *why?*"

"Why?" said Compton defiantly.

"*Because—*" began Briggs but he was unable to add any more as the HOLOGRAPHIC HEAD of Mr Susan Glanville

APPEARED

once again.

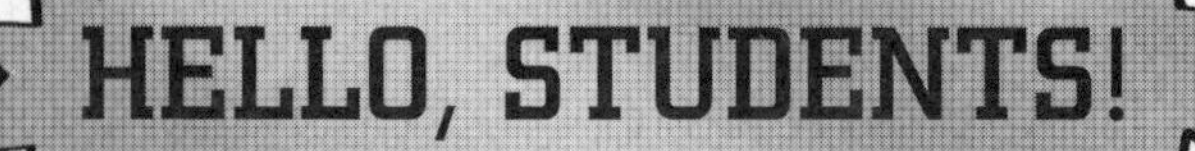

he **bellowed** so **loudly** that Briggs couldn't be heard.

I HAVE AN **EXCITING ANNOUNCEMENT** FOR **YOU**. THIS YEAR'S **GRADUATION DAY** WILL BE *EVEN BETTER* THAN USUAL. A WONDERFUL **NEW EXHIBIT** WILL BE UNVEILED AFTER THIS YEAR'S **GRADUATION CEREMONY**. MORE DETAILS COMING SOON. **SEE YOU THERE. 3.45 P.M. ON THE 22ND AUGUST!**

Scawby Briggs stood for a moment to make **sure** it had finished.

"Right, **where** was I?" he said.

HELLO, STUDENTS!

boomed Mr Susan Glanville *again* while Scawby Briggs fumed at being interrupted again.

I HAVE AN EXCITING ANNOUNCEMENT FOR YOU. THIS YEAR'S GRADUATION DAY WILL BE *EVEN BETTER* THAN USUAL. A WONDERFUL NEW EXHIBIT WILL BE UNVEILED AFTER THIS YEAR'S GRADUATION CEREMONY. MORE DETAILS COMING SOON. SEE YOU THERE. 3.45 P.M. ON THE 22ND AUGUST!

"Okay," Briggs said, getting exceedingly irate. "Perhaps I can finish this ti—"

HELLO, STUDENTS!

thundered Mr Susan Glanville *again*.

Scawby howled and jammed his hands over his ears. Seeing their chance, Compton and Bryan dashed past Briggs and Goxhill, slimed the BRT reader and RACED up into Compton's bedroom.

I HAVE AN **EXCITING ANNOUNCEMENT** FOR **YOU**,

continued the hologram of Mr Susan Glanville.

THIS YEAR'S **GRADUATION DAY** WILL BE *EVEN BETTER* THAN USUAL. A WONDERFUL **NEW EXHIBIT** WILL BE UNVEILED AFTER THIS YEAR'S **GRADUATION CEREMONY**. MORE DETAILS COMING SOON. **SEE YOU THERE.** 3.45 P.M. ON THE **22ND AUGUST!**

"Ooooh," said Goxhill. "That sounded exciting. I wonder what will be unveiled?"

Scawby Briggs hit him **hard** on the arm and stormed off.

Chapter 18

An INVISIBLE DOOR

The next day was Saturday and Samuel Nathaniel Daniels arranged to meet Compton and Bryan in the Eating Zone.

"After what's happened with St Vincent, I thought you could do with a bit of cheering up," he said and, looking around to make sure no one was watching, opened a small, brown bag.

"Thanks," said Compton. "I spent all last night thinking about it. I couldn't concentrate on

at all!"

"Well, stop thinking about it," said Samuel Nathaniel Daniels looking round again as he held open the bag towards Compton and Bryan. "And have one of these instead."

Three ENORMOUS purple bun-like things glistened in the light like they had been bathed in honey and dusted with HUGE crystals of sugar.

"What are THOSE?" said Bryan, his tongue practically falling onto the table.

Sshhhhhhh!

said Samuel Nathaniel Daniels, looking nervously to see if anyone had heard.

If I was found with a bag of Jellied Garys on me in HERE I'd be in serious trouble. They're NOT like the other food they give you, they definitely DO NOT have any of the vitamins and nutrients you'll need for the next five hours. Go on, try one.*

* Jellied Garys were something of a breakfast delicacy for the twenty-seventh century diner. They were created one day after an explosion in a jam factory. A man called Gary was sitting in a nearby park, about to tuck into a sausage roll when it was suddenly covered in a shower of eighty-seven different types of jam from the explosion. The resulting taste sensation of the jam-covered sausage roll was so stickily, tooth-numbingly delicious that Gary immediately set up his own factory and became the RICHEST MAN IN THE WORLD.

Bryan lifted one up to examine it. It felt soft and squidgy and he just *knew* it was going to be delicious. He closed his eyes and sank his teeth into the Jellied Gary.

It was like a

fizzing fairy had set off a thousand FIREWORKS in his mouth.

In precisely four and a half seconds he had polished the **whole thing** off.

"What do you think?" said Samuel Nathaniel Daniels.

"Ghhahhttrrrmmmmssiipppppp," said Bryan who would be **incapable** of recognizable speech for another three minutes.

"He likes it," smiled Compton, biting into his Jellied Gary.

"So, what have you got planned for the weekend then?" said Samuel Nathaniel Daniels once Bryan had recovered from his taste sensation.

"Dunno," said Bryan. "Maybe some **SUPER*FIVES***? Watch some **IAN**?"

"Excellent," said Samuel Nathaniel Daniels. "So you'll be KEEPING AWAY from the old abandoned corridor then?"

Compton looked at Bryan.

he said.

"Oh, you didn't know about the old abandoned corridor?" said Samuel Nathaniel Daniels. "I mustn't say any more about it then. FORGET I said anything."

Compton and Bryan stared silently at Samuel Nathaniel Daniels.

It's just that I thought what with the chat we had yesterday about Gussage St Vincent,

Samuel Nathaniel Daniels said eventually,

that we told you that the lab that he built THE GIGANTUS MACHINE in was down the old abandoned corridor that's just over there.

Compton and Bryan looked round to where Samuel Nathaniel Daniels had indicated and, **sure enough**, there was a door that said,

said Compton.

said Bryan.

"That's because it's INVISIBLE unless it's pointed out by someone with **Level 17 security access**," said Samuel Nathaniel Daniels.

"So if you hadn't mentioned it," said Compton, "then we would NEVER have known about it."

"That's right," said Samuel Nathaniel Daniels, hitting his head with his hand in frustration. "But look, you've got lots of great things to do this weekend. You don't want to be exploring a mysterious but completely off limits, old abandoned corridor, *do you?*"

"Of course not," said Compton.

"We promise," said Bryan.

Ten minutes after Samuel Nathaniel Daniels had left them, Compton and Bryan went back to Compton's room and hatched a plan so BRILLIANT it could speak Welsh.

Rwy'n gynllun gwych.
(I'm a brilliant plan.)

They waited until everyone had GONE to bed and then, under cover of darkness and with only the glow from their InfoTabs to light the way, they crept down the stairs,

out of the PHASE ONE doorway, across the Eating Zone to the door that said,

Then, after a quick look to make sure no one had seen them, they pushed open the door and went inside.

Chapter 19

The MYSTERIOUS Room At The End Of The MYSTERIOUS Corridor

It didn't take long for Compton and Bryan to realize just *why* Samuel Nathaniel Daniels hadn't wanted them to open the door marked,

The corridor beyond was dark and dank and smelled like an old lady who has just had cabbage for tea.

There was a flickering, pale greenish light that came from some bulbs in the ceiling as they *buzzed* on and off. Presently they came to an open doorway with a staircase that led down into gloomy blackness.

"Do you think there's anyone down here?"

said Compton nervously, holding up his InfoTab to try to throw some light into the murkiness of the stairwell.

"Don't be silly," said Bryan, his voice trembling ever so slightly. "You heard Samuel Nathaniel Daniels – this place has been abandoned for years."

And with that, Bryan held up his InfoTab and led the way down the staircase. At the bottom was another corridor, just as dark and dank as the one at the top of the stairs. Except, after their eyes became accustomed to the gloom, Compton thought he saw something.

"What's that?" he said, pointing to the end of the corridor. "Can you see it? Is it a light?"

Bryan squinted and, sure enough, right at the far end of the corridor was a tiny slice of light creeping underneath a door.

And like a couple of **moths** involuntarily drawn to a **flickering bulb**,

Compton and Bryan found themselves walking, **trance-like** down the **corridor** towards it.

When they reached the door that the light was coming from underneath, they **stopped**.

Compton saw a sign above the door and held up his InfoTab to read it. It said

F. A. R. T. ACADEMY
TEST LABORATORY.

"It's the room where St Vincent caused the EXPLOSION when he was an Academy Agent," said Bryan.

"Yeah," gulped Compton and he s l o w l y pushed open the door.

Inside, the LABORATORY was bathed in light from a small lamp on a desk in the corner of the room.

"Someone has been in here," whispered Compton.

There were tubes of funny coloured liquids on shelves, and another door to one side of the room, but what had really caught Compton and Bryan's attention were the walls of the room. They were COVERED in maps.

There were maps of the FPU building, maps of the F. A. R. T. Academy, maps of oceans, maps of sandy islands – in fact, maps of all shapes and sizes. On all the maps were arrows and circles and letters.

"Look at all those," whispered Compton walking over to the maps.

Suddenly they saw a light flick on underneath the door that was at the side of the room and heard someone moving about.

"Quick," whispered Bryan. "We need to go – NOW."

Compton didn't need to be told twice and as quietly but as quickly as they could, the pair left the TEST LABORATORY and SPED up the stairs. They didn't rest until they were safely back in Compton's bedroom.

"Who was that?" asked Compton breathlessly as he and Bryan sat on the edge of his bed.

"I don't know," muttered Bryan shaking his head. "I *thought* that place was supposed to be abandoned."

"We need to go back," said Compton turning his head to look Bryan directly in the eye. "We have to investigate."

Bryan nodded.

"Okay but we'll have to be careful about when we go back," he said. "We can't risk anyone finding out about it."

Compton thought for a moment.

"Next Friday night," he said. "There aren't any lessons the next day so most people sleep in a bit. We can wait until everyone is asleep and then take our time."

"Alright, next Friday it is," agreed Bryan. "But we can't tell anyone we've been down there. If anyone found out we'd be kicked out of the Academy for sure."

As Compton and Bryan discussed their plans, neither had any clue that they wouldn't be able to conduct their investigation next Friday night. You see, sometimes just after you've made a BRILLIANT plan, life has a habit of ripping it up and laughing in your face.

Chapter 20

The Man With The Golden Earring

Thinking that he had heard a noise, the man with a golden earring put the light on in his makeshift store cupboard bedroom and crept into the F. A. R. T. Academy TEST LABORATORY.

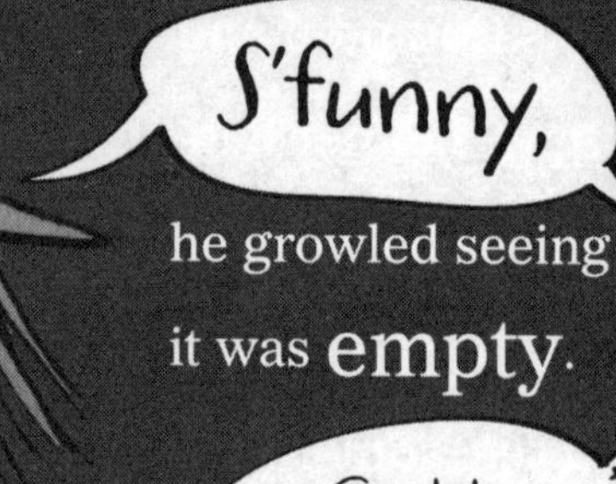

he growled seeing it was empty.

He ran his hand through his long, greasy hair, dialled a number on the palm of his hand and put his thumb in his ear.

"Arrrrrre ye ready?" he said in his low, gruff voice when his call was answered. "Good, good."

He listened and nodded and grunted. Everything seemed to be to his satisfaction.

Arrrrr,

he groaned menacingly.

Just ye be SURE that your information is good. The master needs someone on the inside that he can RELY on, if ye gets me drift.

The man with the golden earring didn't wait for a reply. He took his thumb out of his ear and sat down on the chair by the desk. Pleased with his work, he put his hands behind his head and started to laugh.

HAAAARRRRR HAAARRRRRR HAAAARRRRR.

Unfortunately he was laughing *so hard* and leaning back in his chair *so much* that he ended up falling backwards head over heels out of his chair and onto the **hard** stone floor.

"Arrrrrrrr," he said rubbing his bottom, which had taken the brunt of the fall.

Chapter 21

A HOLOGRAM Called Bryan

Terrified that they would be thrown out of the Academy if anyone found out that they had been in the old abandoned corridor, Compton and Bryan kept their BRILLIANT plan to conduct further investigations to themselves. They spent the next few days playing **SUPER*FIVES***, going to lessons and catching up on the last six hundred and forty-nine years of ACTION MOVIES.*

* On reflection, Compton thought that his favourite movie was *Top Flight*, a high-octane action adventure film about a man who was the world's number one darts player by day and an international spy by night. It was widely thought that *Top Flight 59: Treble Twenty Double Agent* was easily the best movie EVER made.

On Thursday morning after another horrific twenty-seventh century breakfast, Compton, Bryan and the rest of the PHASE ONE Academy Agents followed a NaviBot to their first lesson of the day, HISTORIC TIME MACHINES. Today, their usual teacher, Mr Bobson, was off sick and so he had arranged for the class to spend the morning in the F. A. R. T. Academy Time Museum. After a few minutes of snaking through maze-like corridors, the NaviBot eventually came to a stop outside an ENORMOUS metal door.

"WE ARE HERE," the **NaviBot** said in its MECHANICAL VOICE before moving up to the door and knocking three times. A tiny eyehole slid open for a moment and then just as quickly SLAMMED SHUT.

After a few moments of silence, a series of ENORMOUS metallic clunks and clangs could be heard coming from behind the HUGE door, like a lot of very heavy locks were being undone.

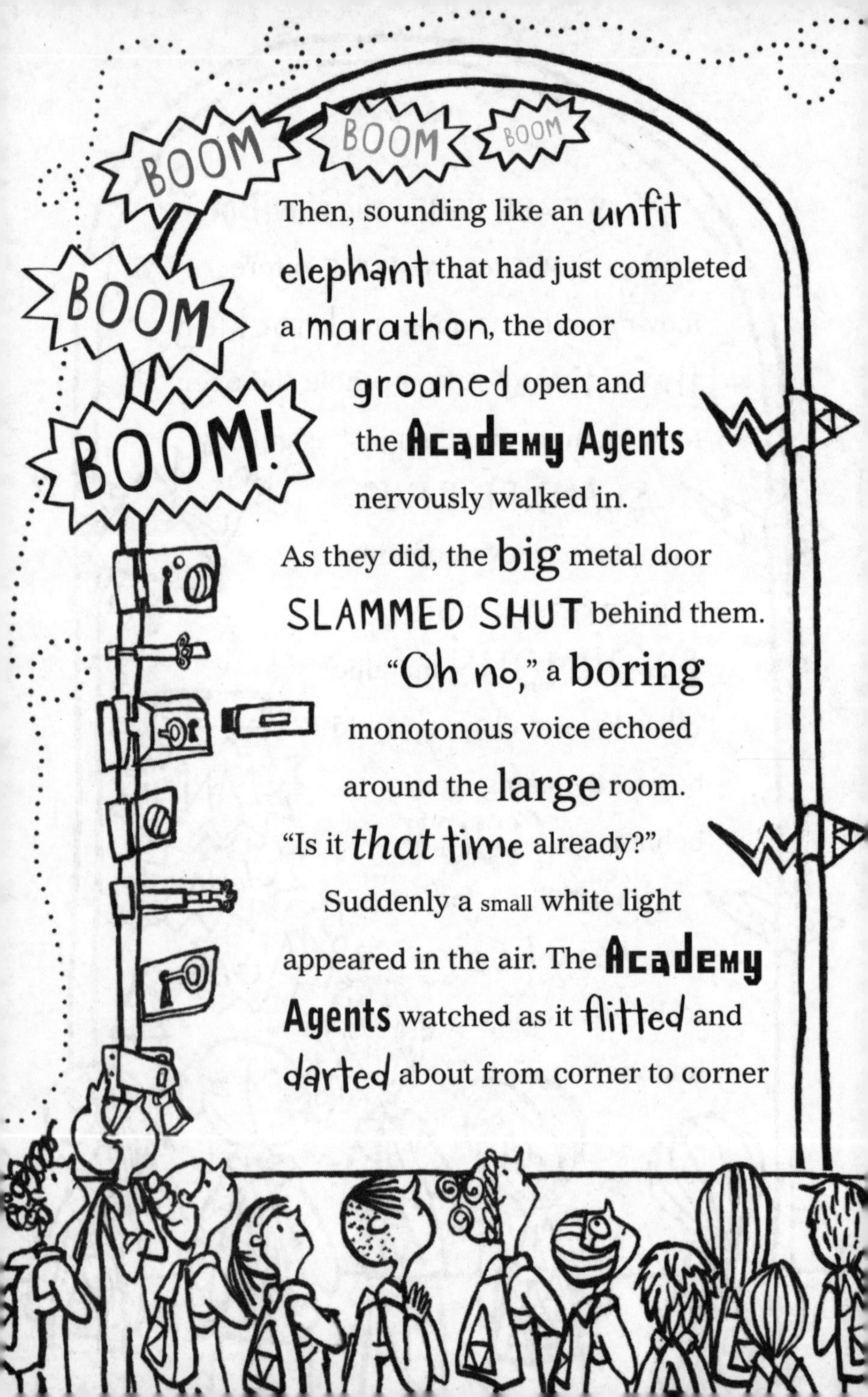

Then, sounding like an unfit elephant that had just completed a marathon, the door groaned open and the Academy Agents nervously walked in.

As they did, the big metal door SLAMMED SHUT behind them.

"Oh no," a boring monotonous voice echoed around the large room. "Is it *that time* already?"

Suddenly a small white light appeared in the air. The **Academy Agents** watched as it flitted and darted about from corner to corner for a few moments before becoming larger and BRIGHTER and floating down to the floor beside them.

As it got nearer and nearer, Compton could see that the light was turning into a man with long brown hair and a goatee beard,* or at least the light was turning into a HOLOGRAM of a man with long brown hair and a goatee beard.*

* Goatee beards are those beards that look like you have put a load of glue on someone's upper lip and chin and then dipped their face in a bin. They were briefly fashionable between the hours of 9 a.m. and 3 p.m. on Monday 6th of May 1991 but have remained inexplicably popular among magicians and computer programmers ever since.

"Good morning, class," said the HOLOGRAM drearily. "Not that I EVER have a very good morning, what with me being a three-dimensional image created by a series of light beams and so unable to experience good days or bad days."

The HOLOGRAM sighed.

"Ah well, I suppose we should get the lesson started. The sooner we start, the sooner we'll be finished and then I'll NEVER have to see any of you again. Now then, could someone go over to the coat hooks on the wall and push the fifteenth one from the left?"

Lola walked over to the wall that the HOLOGRAM had pointed to, found the fifteenth coat hook from the left and pushed hard. As she did, two big glass boxes s l o w l y rose up in the middle of the room and around them, hundreds of criss-crossed red beams of light hummed and crackled.

"Wow," said Bryan, who loved a thing rising out of the ground more than just about any other human on earth.*

* Bryan's list of favourite things that rise out of the ground are as follows: bollards, rock stars, a car his dad had once shown him on the internet, zombies, fountains and trees (although he wasn't very happy about how long they took about it!).

"By the way, my name is Bryan," continued the HOLOGRAM. "But you can call me HoloBryan."

"Cool, my name's Bryan too," said Bryan, marvelling at the extraordinary coincidence of two people sharing the same name, in the same room, at the same time.

"I know," said HoloBryan. "I was named after you."

At that point in TIME, if someone could have offered Bryan Nylon's brain an opportunity of a fortnight's walking holiday in the Peak District, then it would have taken it, *no question*.

"But how," said Compton. "You've *only just* met."

"After you two SAVED THE UNIVERSE," droned on HoloBryan, "it was decided to rename me in Bryan's honour. I *used* to be called Colin."*

"Wow," said Compton. "That's really cool."

"To be honest," continued HoloBryan in his lifeless way, "it's been downhill ever since. Now then, please **pay attention**. Due to Mr Bobson's recent illness, I shall be your teacher today for HISTORIC TIME MACHINES."

"Er, excuse me, HoloBryan?" said Compton, putting up his hand.

"Yes?" said HoloBryan.

"Er, well," said Compton. "I **don't** want to sound rude, but *why* are you a HOLOGRAM? *Why* don't we have a teacher who is, well, alive?"

* After Compton and Bryan had SAVED THE UNIVERSE, a committee decided that to commemorate such a momentous achievement they would rename Colin after Bryan and rename cheese and onion crisps after Compton.

HoloBryan floated towards the glass boxes.

"I am a HOLOGRAM simply because the contents of The Time Museum are very, very precious indeed. As most of you will know, there are certain FPU agents who have the authority to TRAVEL backwards and forwards through TIME. For this they use their Wrist Activated Time CHangers."

A murmur of agreement swept through the Academy Agents.

"Well," continued HoloBryan, "those W.A.T.CH.es are the only TIME-TRAVEL MACHINES within the whole of the FPU. Apart from these."

With that HoloBryan turned towards the glass boxes and as he did, the red beams of light that surrounded them DISAPPEARED.

These ITEMS that you see before you are the two earliest examples of TIME MACHINES EVER invented. BOTH are in perfect working order and can take someone BACK IN TIME. It is because they are in FULL operational condition that the FPU have employed the services of a HOLOGRAM to curate **The Time Museum**. We had some trouble a few years ago when a human was cleaning them and accidentally sent himself hurtling BACK THROUGH TIME. After THAT it was decided that only NON-humans should work in here.

HoloBryan floated over to the first of the big glass boxes and the **Academy Agents** followed him.

"In here," he said so miserably that you'd think he'd just been told that he had to have his bottom removed, "is Stinky Trevor, the second oldest TIME MACHINE ever created."*

In contrast to its strange name, Stinky Trevor looked absolutely BEAUTIFUL. It resembled a kind of old-fashioned shop till and was mostly made of brass and silver. Everywhere you looked were buttons and levers and dials and switches.

* Stinky Trevor was named after Trevor Augustus Remington III. He started to build the time machine in the year 2089 and claimed that he wouldn't wash again until he had finished it. He completed his machine in 2094, by which time he had also broken Stenchy Wendy's World's Smelliest Human record.

"Stinky Trevor is set to take the operator back to just one specific TIME PERIOD," continued HoloBryan cheerlessly. "Pull the golden lever and you'll TRAVEL BACK IN TIME twenty-thousand years. We have no idea why it was set for that particular time because Stinky Trevor's creator only took one TRIP THROUGH TIME, where he was eaten by a sabre-toothed tiger, which itself was then trodden on by a woolly mammoth."

HoloBryan floated over to the second glass box.

"And this," he said gloomily and with no fanfare whatsoever, "is the oldest TIME MACHINE ever created."

The **Academy Agents** peered into the glass box.

"There's **NOTHING** there," said Hector. "It's *empty*."

"Yes, it's a bit like *my life* really," said HoloBryan sadly. "The *oldest* **TIME MACHINE in HISTORY** will be placed in its glass cabinet at a special unveiling after the **F. A. R. T. Academy GRADUATION CEREMONY**."

"So *that's* what Mr Susan Glanville has been going on about," said Hector.

"So what *is* the *oldest* **TIME MACHINE in HISTORY**?" said Compton eagerly.

HoloBryan rolled his eyes.

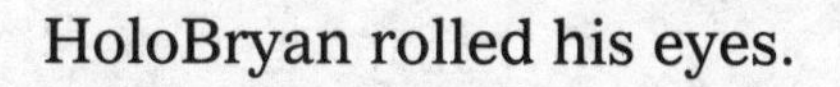

"Your sandwich, of course," he said. "You two created the

OLDEST TIME MACHINE in HISTORY."

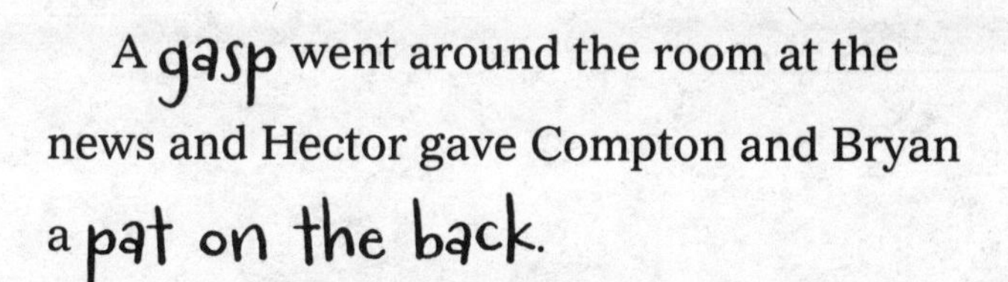

A gasp went around the room at the news and Hector gave Compton and Bryan a pat on the back.

"Nice one," he said. "That's pretty IMPRESSIVE."

"Now, if you'll excuse me," said HoloBryan, flickering a little, "I know I said that all days are the same but this one has been particularly terrible and I need to go and recharge."

The glass boxes s l o w l y began to lower themselves into the floor and as they did, HoloBryan DISAPPEARED.

Actually, it was a bit of a shame that HoloBryan didn't stay for a bit longer because he would have seen something that had NEVER happened before. The whole of **The Time Museum** started flashing and an alarm began howling overhead. Suddenly, the big metal door opened and into the room walked Mr Susan Glanville and Ms Drimpton.

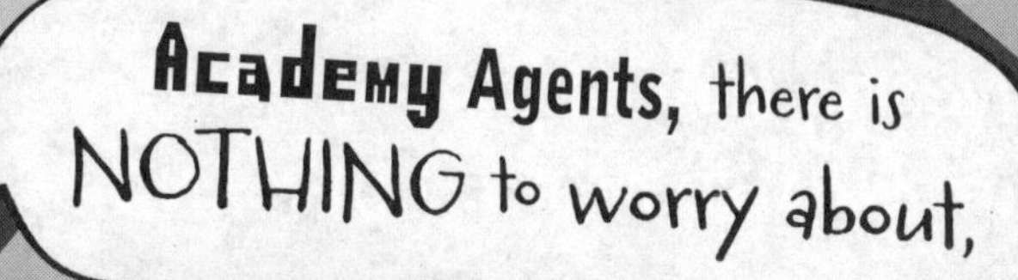

said Mr Susan Glanville reassuringly.

Please follow Ms Drimpton back to the PHASE ONE Zone where she will give you further instructions.

An excited chatter started to bubble and froth inside **The Time Museum**.

"I don't remember telling any of you slavering nosebags to start talking," squawked Ms Drimpton. "I DEMAND silence!"

The excited chatter spluttered and coughed and then died.

"Follow me, you clattering goggleheads, and be quick about it," she screeched and started to march her way down the corridor. "COME ON!"

The Academy Agents began to file out of The Time Museum and follow Ms Drimpton. As Compton and Bryan were about to leave, Mr Susan Glanville stopped them both.

Chapter 22

In A Cubicle, In A Toilet, Where It ALL Began

Once outside **The Time Museum**, things started to move pretty quickly for Compton and Bryan. A very worried-looking Samuel Nathaniel Daniels stood flanked by four **FPU Special Agents**.

"There's not much time," he said urgently as he ushered them down the corridor. "Gussage St Vincent has ESCAPED."

"WHAT?" said Compton, turning to Mr Susan Glanville. "But you said that was IMPOSSIBLE."

"I know," said Mr Susan Glanville, looking worried.

"What about the steel-lined cell with laser bars on the walls?" said Compton.

"I know," nodded Mr Susan Glanville.

"And the three lava-filled moats?" said Bryan.

"I know," said Mr Susan Glanville.

"And the lava-resistant electric eels in the lava-filled moats," added Compton.

"I know," said Mr Susan Glanville.

"And the cell being buried four hundred metres below ground level," said Bryan.

said Mr Susan Glanville.

"And the Dungeon of Infinity," said Compton. "What about that?"

"I know," said Mr Susan Glanville. "I know, I know, I know, I know. We simply don't know HOW he managed it."

"But in the meantime we need to get you somewhere safe," said Samuel Nathaniel Daniels. "Just in case he comes here looking for you."

Compton and Bryan looked shocked.

It's ONLY for a few days,

said Samuel Nathaniel Daniels.

If Gussage St Vincent is after YOU, Compton, then you'll be completely safe back home. I happen to know that he absolutely HATES the twenty-first century and he wouldn't set foot in it in a MILLION YEARS.* Besides, we've sent a team of FPU agents ahead to guard you. They're BRILLIANTLY disguised and will blend in effortlessly with twenty-first century life. You WON'T know they're there but they'll make sure you're okay.

* Gussage St Vincent's hatred of the twenty-first century began in 2632 when he returned to the year 2007 only to discover that the moustache had gone out of fashion several years earlier. He vowed there and then never to return to a century who treated upper lip facial hair with such disdain.

It didn't take long for the four of them to reach Departures.

"What's going to happen?" said Compton, looking more nervous than he had in his whole life.

"Don't worry," said Samuel Nathaniel Daniels, placing a hand on Compton's shoulder. "It'll only be for a short time, just until we can be sure it's safe here. GRADUATION DAY is two months away, there'll be plenty of time to catch up. I'll send you back to The Burger Shack toilets."

And with that he pushed some buttons on his **W.A.T.CH.** and Compton and Bryan saw the air around them

crackle

and

fizz.

When the air
around them stopped
crackling
they saw that they
were back in the toilet of
The Burger Shack.
They heard the door outside
s l o w l y squeak open.

they heard Compton's dad call nervously.

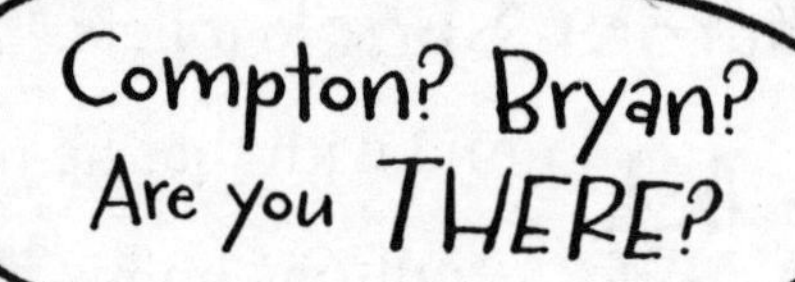

Compton pulled the cubicle door open and nearly fell out.

"Compton," said his father, looking very strangely at the pair of them.

"Are you guys okay? Where are your clothes? What are you doing in those weird red onesies?"

Compton looked at his father and nearly burst into tears. He grabbed and hugged him as hard as he could.

"Dad," he said, gripping him tightly. "It's so good to see you again."

"*Again?*" said Mr Valance, letting the hug go and looking at his son. "You've only been GONE for a few minutes."

"Oh, er, yes," said Compton nervously. "Yes, that's right – a *few minutes!*"

Chapter 23

The Switcheroo

As they walked out of the toilets and back to their seats, Compton and Bryan worriedly scanned The Burger Shack.

Despite Samuel Nathaniel Daniels's assurance that Gussage St Vincent wouldn't come after them in the twenty-first century, all their senses were on HIGH ALERT.

At one table they saw a family enjoying a meal, at another a young couple smiling weirdly at each other, and at another table there seemed to be what looked like a birthday party taking place. At least, Compton guessed it was a birthday party on account of there being three people dressed as pirates standing around as a cake was delivered. Bryan nudged Compton and pointed to another table.

"Didn't Mr Susan Glanville say the FPU agents would be impossible to *recognize?*" he said, sniggering.

In the corner of The Burger Shack were four people dressed in tight silver suits and tiny bowler hats. EVERY single one of them was peering at Compton and Bryan around an uʍop-ǝpᴉsdn menu.

"That really is rubbish," scoffed Compton as they sat down and continued the starters and Zillion-Dollar Shakes that they had ordered over two weeks earlier.

"What on earth happened to you two in that toilet?" said Mr Valance looking at Compton and Bryan's red onesies. "I mean I *know* you two were bored but I didn't think it had come to dressing up in toilets!"

Compton **thought** about telling the truth but *how* could you possibly explain to your dad that you had just spent the last few weeks in a secret **training facility** over six hundred years in the FUTURE and that right now THE UNIVERSE's most deadly time crim was HUNTING *you down?*

"Oh, er, nothing," he said eventually.

Mr Valance had the feeling that if he asked any more questions then he might discover something that he **definitely** didn't want to hear. So he quickly changed the subject and began talking about a rather excellent episode of

BADGER! STOAT! ACTION!

that he had seen on TV the night before.*

Once the meal was finished, Mr Valance drove them to Bryan's house.

"See you tomorrow?" said Compton.

"Sure thing," said Bryan. "It'll be fun to do some normal stuff again."

* BADGER! STOAT! ACTION! was the brilliant and hilarious show where people sent in home footage of badgers and stoats doing crazy and funny things.

Compton stared out of the car window for the rest of the journey back home.

EVERY few minutes he saw another terribly disguised FPU agent following them. He saw one in a field pretending to be a scarecrow.*

He saw one in a pram pretending to be a baby.**

He even saw one just standing on the pavement outside a shop.***

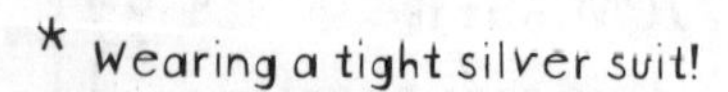

* Wearing a tight silver suit!

** Wearing a tight silver suit!

*** You've guessed it, this agent was also wearing a tight silver suit.

Compton assumed that *this one* must have been pretending to be a **lamppost** as a dog wandered over and did a **wee** up his leg.

When he got back to **Morlock Cottage**, the first thing Compton heard was his brother **Bravo**. Well, more the *sound* of his brother singing **cheerfully**.*

Lah dee de de dah...dum dum de dum

* Since a bizarre time-travel incident involving Bravo, frogspawn and a home-made chocolate cake, Compton's brother liked nothing more than singing along to medieval folk songs with his girlfriend Nancy Flowers. If you think that's weird, you should have seen what he was like BEFORE the bizarre time-travel incident involving frogspawn and a home-made chocolate cake!

Compton realized that he had missed his family more than he thought and so after quickly changing out of his red onesie and into some normal twenty-first century clothes, he found his mum and gave her a great BIG squeeze.

"What's that for?" said Mrs Valance, quite surprised at this sudden display of affection.

"Oh, nothing," said Compton. "I just missed you, that's all."

"You silly sausage," said his mum. "I only saw you this morning."

Compton didn't say anything. He just gave his mum another hug.

"So, I was thinking," said Mrs Valance, "I *know* you've been out for lunch today but I'm a bit busy to cook tonight so how about we order some Chinese takeaway instead?"

"BRILLIANT idea!" said Compton eagerly and went upstairs to his bedroom dreaming of duck pancakes and plum sauce. But as soon as he shut the door behind him, the air in his bedroom crackled and fizzed and Samuel Nathaniel Daniels

APPEARED.

"What?" said Compton. "That was quick! Have you caught Gussage?"

"Not yet," said Samuel Nathaniel Daniels. "But it won't be long now. We have increased security at the Academy and so it's COMPLETELY safe for you two to come back and finish your PHASE ONE TRAINING."

"Oh great," said Compton half-heartedly.

"Something wrong?" said Samuel Nathaniel Daniels.

"Well," said Compton, "it's just that I didn't realize how much I missed everyone. My mum and dad, I mean."

Samuel Nathaniel Daniels smiled.

"And we're having Chinese food for tea," said Compton. "It's *sort of* my favourite."

"Tell you what then," said Samuel Nathaniel Daniels, pushing some buttons on his W.A.T.CH, "why don't I pick you up tomorrow morning instead? I'll be here at eight o'clock."

"Great, thanks," said Compton as the air in Compton's bedroom crackled and fizzed and Samuel Nathaniel Daniels

DISAPPEARED.

The next morning, Compton woke up with a lovely full feeling in his tummy from the CRISPY duck pancakes, the sticky plum sauce and the noodles that he'd eaten the night before. He got up, had a wash and brushed his teeth, and sat in his bedroom and waited. To be honest it was a *bit* strange being in a bedroom where you didn't have to keep avoiding things flying out of the wall.

In fact, the more Compton sat there,

the more he looked forward to getting back

to the twenty-seventh century.

At eight o'clock exactly

the air in Compton's → 8.00 a.m.

bedroom crackled

and fizzed and Samuel Nathaniel Daniels

APPEARED again.

"Right then," he said. "All set?"

Compton nodded.

"Have you been to see Bryan yet?" he said.

"Agent Hendrix is picking him up now," said Samuel Nathaniel Daniels, pressing the buttons on his W.A.T.C.H. "We'll meet up with him at the Academy."

A second later, the air inside Compton's bedroom crackled and fizzed and the pair

DISAPPEARED.

When the air around him stopped crackling and fizzing, Compton immediately recognized the hustle and bustle of ARRIVALS.

"Come on," said Samuel Nathaniel Daniels, walking over to a REGISTRATION DESK. "Let's get you checked back in."

Suddenly, Agent Hendrix came RUSHING up to them.

"*Gone?*" repeated Compton.

"What do you *mean*, Agent Hendrix?" said Samuel Nathaniel Daniels.

"When I arrived at his house for the pick-up," said Agent Hendrix, "Academy Agent Nylon was NOWHERE to be seen. But I found this on his bed."

Agent Hendrix held up a small golden card that had the initials

stamped on it in elaborate lettering.

said Samuel Nathaniel Daniels.

Chapter 24

The Ransom Demand

A stinky, sweaty, stubbly man wearing a golden earring threw Bryan into the corner of a dark, dank room

"You'll never get away with THIS!" said Bryan, bravely hiding his fear as best he could.

BE QUIET, ye swab!

ordered the sweaty man.

Ain't NOBODY going to find ye down here.

"What do you want?" said Bryan, looking nervously round at his new surroundings.

"I'll let the master tell you that h'self," said the horrible, stubbly man. "He'll be here faster than a parrot can find a treasure chest."

The man with the golden earring laughed a rough, DEEP, terrifying laugh and stood with his back against the wall of the room. Suddenly the door next to him BANGED open and a man with a white wig, a red jacket and an outrageous moustache burst into the room.

My dear, dear Bryan Nylon, he said. How WONDERFUL to finally meet you.

Gussage St Vincent, said Bryan, immediately recognizing the man.

"The very same," he said, nodding his head and flashing his mouth full of silver teeth.

WHAT do you want? said Bryan angrily. WHERE am I?

Ha ha haha ah ah ah aaaahhh!

Gussage St Vincent laughed.

"What you are doing here will become obvious very shortly," he sneered. "Where you are I shan't say, but I can tell you when you are. You are in the year 2662."

"2662?" repeated Bryan. "But I don't understand. I didn't join the F. A. R. T. Academy until 2664."

"Precisely," laughed Gussage St Vincent, tossing back his head and flicking his ENORMOUS white wig over his shoulder. "No one will EVER think to look for you two years ago!

It's a perfectly BRILLIANT plan!"

Bryan looked around the room. It was dark but there was something familiar about it. Something he couldn't *quite* put his finger on.

Gussage St Vincent then turned to the stubbly man.

"Tell me," he asked quietly, "did EVERYTHING go according to plan?"

Arrrrrr, as SURE as the crows fly from Devil's Island on the night of the third full moon of the year,

said the stubbly man.

"Good, good," said St Vincent, rubbing his hands in delight.

"And tell me, how does my moustache look?"

"Arrrrrrr," said the stubbly man. "MAGNIFICENT, my master."

"Oh, do you think so?" said St Vincent, running his hands through his upper-lip hair in delight. "Do you think it's bushy enough?"

"As sure as the gems nestlin' in Queen Isabella's crown sparkle like the water round Hangman's Cove," said the stubbly man.

said Gussage St Vincent.

"Because you **know** I like to look good and **all** this scheming and kidnapping takes up *so much* of my time—"

"Beverley," said Bryan suddenly. "Your name is *Beverley?*"

"Er, it be a boy's name too," said Beverley, a little defensively.

"Really?" said Bryan, smiling. "Because **I** don't know *any* boys called Beverley. I know a woman who works at the supermarket. *Her* name is Beverley. And I know a woman who does yoga with my mum. *Her* name is Beverley. And then there's my dad's great-aunt. *Her* name is Beverley. And—"

"ENOUGH!" yelled Gussage St Vincent. "You are **not** here to mock my men and their ladynames."

Bryan stopped laughing and looked around the room again. There was something about it that was gnawing away at his memory. Something not in the room but outside the room that was

flashing through his brain.

Or maybe not flashing...maybe it was spluttering like a flickering light.

"So what am *I* here for then?" said Bryan.

"You are here to record a message," said Gussage St Vincent. "I have kidnapped you and will ask for a *lot* of money for your safe return. You will record a message that will let the **FPU** know exactly where and when they can find you in exchange for all that lovely booty."

"A message?" said Bryan suspiciously. "That's all?"

"That's all," said Gussage St Vincent kindly. "If they cough up the cash, you go free, and if they don't then

Bryan swallowed nervously.

"Right then," said St Vincent, suddenly producing a piece of paper from his top pocket. He held his stolen W.A.T.C.H. up to Bryan like a video camera. "If you can say this while I film you, that would be wonderful."

As Gussage St Vincent pushed the record button on the W.A.T.C.H. and shouted,

ACTION!

Bryan looked at the piece of paper with the ransom message that he had just been given. Like a flickering light in his mind suddenly coming on full beam, he finally realized exactly *where* he was.

Once the message had been recorded, Gussage St Vincent pushed a few buttons on the W.A.T.C.H.

"There," he said. "Now that's just been sent two years into the FUTURE to the FPU."

A moment passed and a little noise **bleeped** from the **W.A.T.CH.** to indicate that the message had been sent. Gussage St Vincent looked at Beverley and started laughing in a really weird, crazy way. And when he started to laugh in a weird, crazy way then Beverley started to laugh in a weird, crazy way too.

"What's so *funny*?" asked Bryan nervously.

"Well, I'm not *really* interested in the ransom at all," said Gussage St Vincent, chuckling. "I just needed you to create a little diversion so that I can get on with my

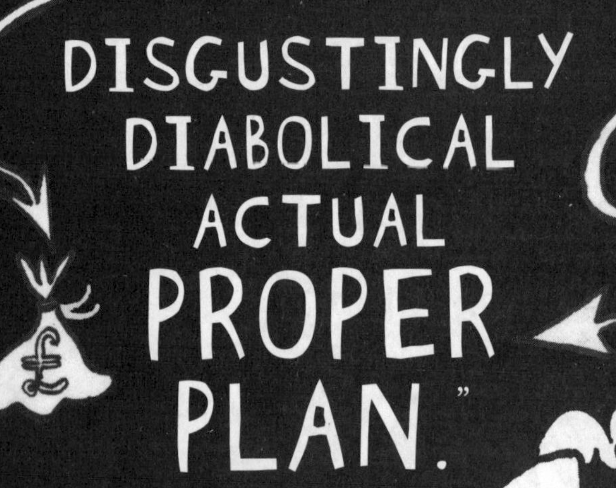

HA HA HA HA
HAAAAAAAAAAAR!

Chapter 25

The MASTER Of TIME

Bryan waited patiently for the sinister, taking-over-THE-UNIVERSE type laughing to stop.

"So you didn't kidnap me for the money?" he said finally.

"No, no, no, no, no, no," said Gussage St Vincent, wiping away the tears from his eyes. "I don't care about that at all."

And with that he started laughing again, slapping Beverley on the back as he did.

"So what did you want then?" said Bryan, just a little bit confused. "Why did you need a diversion?"

"Well," said Gussage once he had regained his composure, "I want to get my hands on something much, much, much *more* valuable than money or jewels and I don't want that idiot Nathaniel Daniels or any other FPU agents getting in my way. I want to steal that TIME-TRAVELLING SANDWICH of yours."

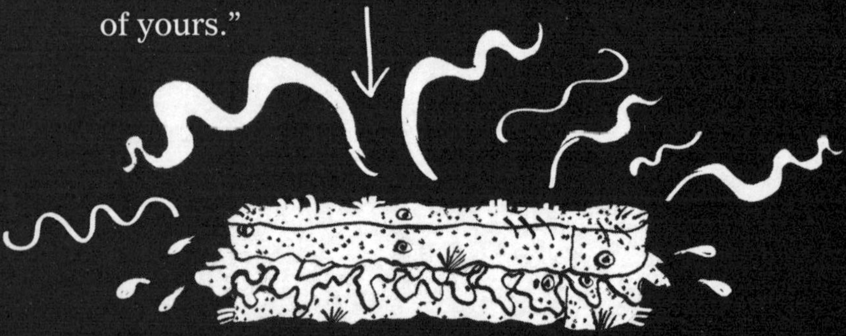

"What?" said Bryan. "*Why* do you need the sandwich?"

"Because your sandwich is very, *very* special," said Gussage St Vincent, prowling around the room.

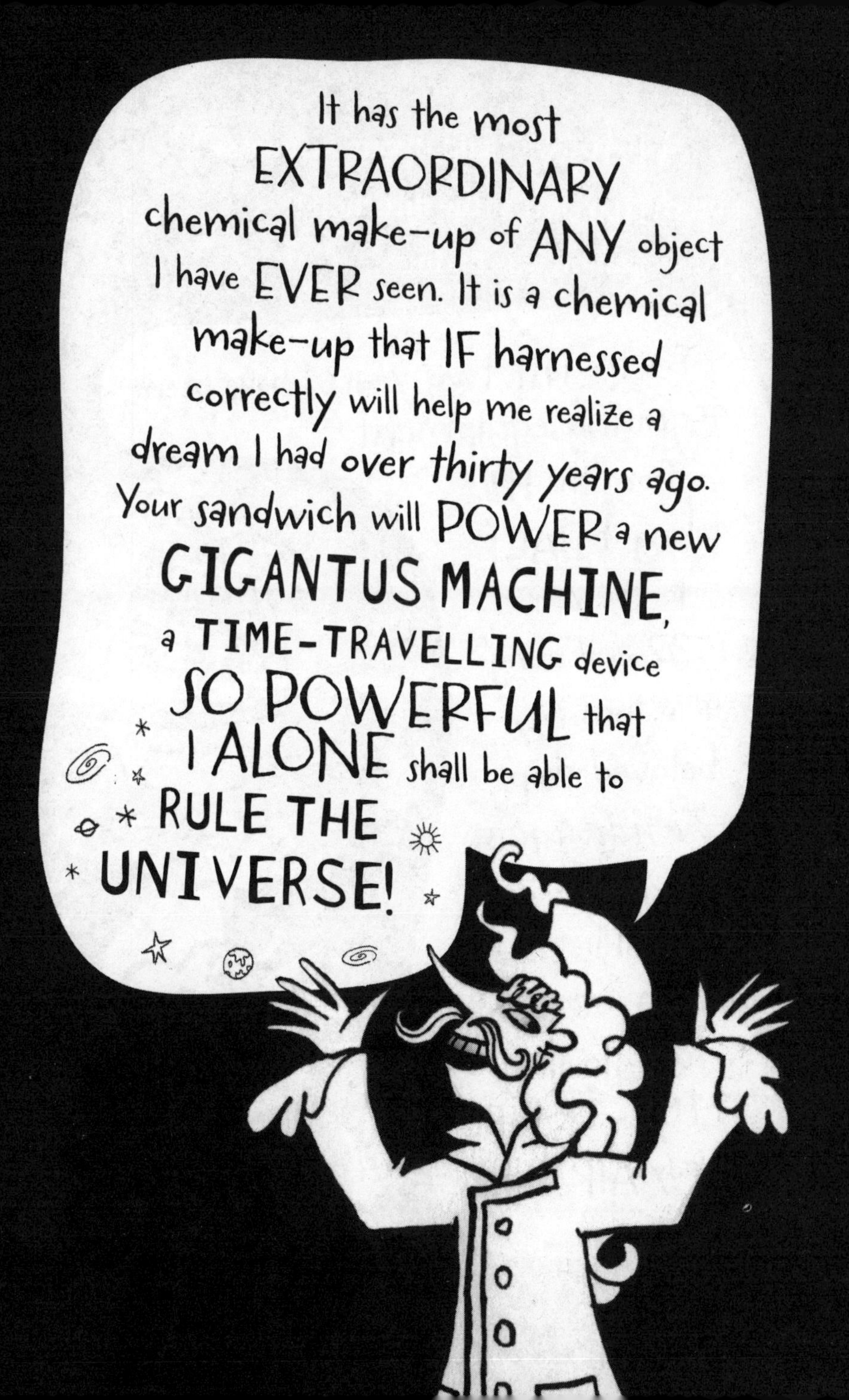
It has the most EXTRAORDINARY chemical make-up of ANY object I have EVER seen. It is a chemical make-up that IF harnessed correctly will help me realize a dream I had over thirty years ago. Your sandwich will POWER a new GIGANTUS MACHINE, a TIME-TRAVELLING device SO POWERFUL that I ALONE shall be able to RULE THE UNIVERSE!

"H-how?" said Bryan, just a teeny bit disturbed at the direction this conversation was taking.

For the last two years I have been acquiring equipment from the **FPU**, taking it BACK to the year 1732 and using it to turn my beloved ship, *Fandango's Revenge*, from a humble pirate galleon into a fully functioning, TIME-TRAVEL ready AIRSHIP.

Once I have the sandwich I will take it back and fit it into a power unit that I have recently installed in *Fandango's* supply room. The ship will then be able to take me to ANY moment in the past or FUTURE and to ANY point in space. I will become the **MASTER OF TIME** and NOTHING will be able to STOP me. HA HA HA HAAAAAAAAAR.

I WON'T HELP YOU,

shouted Bryan.

"Oh, you *already* have," said St Vincent.

"I have already sent this ransom message of yours, which will bring the FPU to a specific place and time to collect you once they have paid the ransom. They will of course pay up to get you back and set a trap to catch me."

Gussage St Vincent stroked his chin and smirked.

"Obviously they will fail to do so because I won't be where you just told them to go," he said.

"Huh," said Bryan just a teensy bit confused.

"Oh come on, it's simple," groaned Gussage as he whipped out a piece of paper and a pen from his pocket and started drawing a diagram of his plan. "At the exact moment that all the FPU agents are waiting to catch me, I will actually be at your F. A. R. T. Academy GRADUATION CEREMONY stealing the TIME MACHINE SANDWICH *before* it can be placed in **The Time Museum**. *No one* will be able to stop me and I shall become, as I think I already just pointed out, the

MASTER OF TIME!

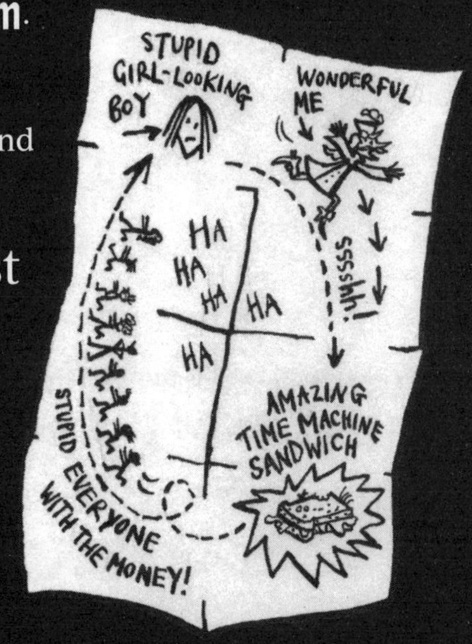

HA HA HA HAAAAAAAAAAAAA!"*

* It had taken Gussage St Vincent nearly nine months to come up with the name "MASTER OF TIME" and so he intended to use it as often as he could.**

** Other names that Gussage had thought of and then rejected had been: THE TIME MAN, THE MAN WHO CONTROLLED TIME, THE CONTROLLER OF TIME, THE COMMANDER OF TIME, THE CAPTAIN OF TIME, THE PRINCE OF TIME, THE KING OF TIME, MR TIME, THE T MAN, KING T MAN, KING T, T, and KEV.

And with that, Gussage St Vincent and Beverley flounced out of the room, SLAMMING the door and laughing all the while. Then the door opened and Gussage St Vincent came back in.

"Sorry," he said. "I FORGOT something."

He picked up a piece of paper that was lying on a desk in the corner of the room, started laughing again and flounced out again.

Once he was certain St Vincent and Beverley weren't coming back, Bryan quickly fell to his knees and started looking in the dust and the dirt on the floor of the room. You see, what Gussage St Vincent and Beverley *didn't know* was that during the time that it had taken Gussage to reveal the details of his

Bryan's brain had been working overtime and had, for the second time in his life, put together a

PRETTY FANTASTIC WHOPPING GREAT PLAN OF ACTUAL WONDROUSNESS ITSELF.*

After a few moments of frantic searching he found what he was looking for: a small stone with a pointy edge. It was perfect. Bryan just hoped he had enough time to put his plan into action.

* The first time Bryan's brain had come up with such a plan had been when he was six and he had had the notion of putting his underpants in the freezer on hot days to cool him down. That wasn't the brilliant plan, by the way, the brilliant plan was when he opened the freezer to get them out and his brain thought it would actually be a ridiculous idea to wear frozen underpants and so he shut the freezer drawer and walked away. In fact, as far as he knows, the pants are still there, underneath a packet of fish fingers.

Chapter 26

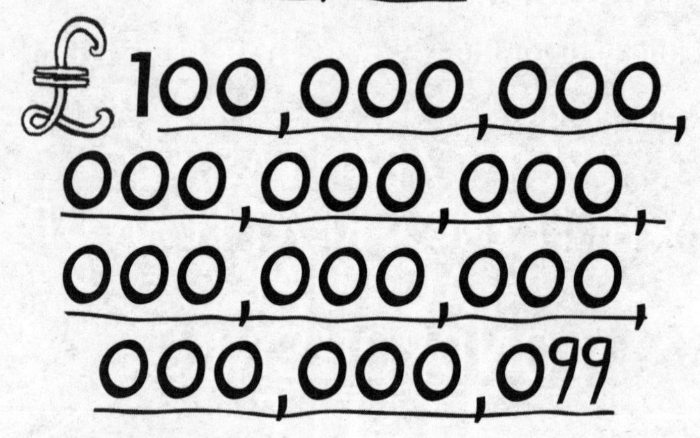

In a secret room in the FPU HQ, hidden behind a door marked

WOMEN'S TOILETS OUT OF ORDER,

The Commissioner, Samuel Nathaniel Daniels, Mr Susan Glanville and Compton all stood watching the GIANT HOLOGRAPHIC face of Bryan Nylon *looming* over them.*

"This message was sent to us half an hour ago," said The Commissioner.

I am unharmed,

said Bryan in a **ROBOTIC, MONOTONE VOICE** as he read from a piece of paper in front of him.

As you will see, I have been KIDNAPPED by the majestic and glorious Gussage St Vincent, and am being kept hostage until a ransom is paid.

Bryan looked nervously off camera at whoever was doing the filming.

* Just so we're clear, this is the holographic face of the real Bryan Nylon and not the holographic face of the Time Museum curator, HoloBryan. To be fair, when the committee decided to honour Bryan Nylon by renaming Colin the hologram after him, they hadn't imagined the present situation ever arising. If they had they might have honoured Bryan in a different way by naming a building or a type of newt after him or something.

Go on, came a whisper. Read the rest.

If you pay the ransom, in FULL, at the agreed time and location, then I will remain unharmed and will be freed,

read Bryan before he put down the piece of paper and added casually,

Freed from this secret, dark, dank room with flickering lights outside.

Suddenly the ENORMOUS and stupendously moustached HOLOGRAPHIC face of Gussage St Vincent APPEARED.

Nylon will NOT be harmed,
he said quietly,
just so long as YOU follow my instructions. The ransom is ONE HUNDRED HUNDRED HUNDRED HUNDRED BILLION BILLION BILLION and NINETY-NINE EARTH POUNDS. YOU will bring it to a secret location at 3.45 p.m. on 22nd August, 2664. I will be in touch in due course to let YOU know where YOU need to bring the money. Until then, goodbye.

The HOLOGRAM DISAPPEARED.

"Isn't 22nd August graduation day?" said Compton.

"Yes it is," said Mr Susan Glanville. "But *where* are we going to find ONE HUNDRED HUNDRED HUNDRED HUNDRED HUNDRED BILLION BILLION BILLION and NINETY-NINE EARTH POUNDS?"

"We've got to," said Samuel Nathaniel Daniels. "Bryan's LIFE might depend on it."

"Don't worry," said The Commissioner. "We don't really *need* to get the money. As soon as St Vincent tells us *where* the secret location is, we can just send **FPU Special Agents** BACK IN TIME to lie in wait for him there. Once he arrives at the scene we'll arrest him."

"BRILLIANT!" said Mr Susan Glanville. "That's a wonderful idea."

"It's *so* simple," marvelled Samuel Nathaniel Daniels.

"Then why hasn't St Vincent thought of it?" said Compton suspiciously. "He seems pretty clever to me. After all, he managed to escape from your super-duper, top security prison with lava moats and the Dungeon of Infinity, didn't he?"

"Er, well..." said The Commissioner.

"And he tricked you into thinking that he was after me instead of Bryan," continued Compton.

"I think—" began Samuel Nathaniel Daniels.

"That's just the problem," said Compton. "You don't think *enough!*"

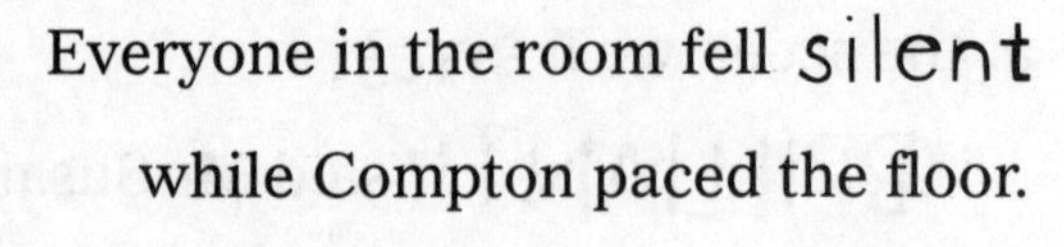

Everyone in the room fell silent while Compton paced the floor.

"That message," he said suddenly. "Can you play part of it again?"

"Well, yes," said Samuel Nathaniel Daniels. "Thanks to the new VOICE-ACTIVATED, HIGH-SPEED, FULLY AUTOMATIC—"

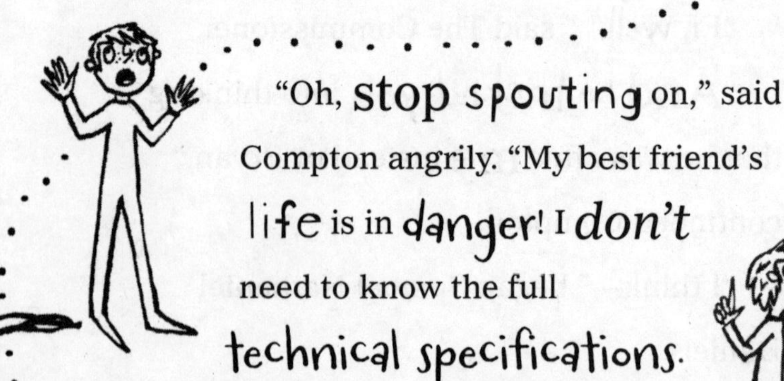

"Oh, stop spouting on," said Compton angrily. "My best friend's life is in danger! I *don't* need to know the full technical specifications. Play the bit again just before the moment when St Vincent comes in."

"Er, point alpha twenty-three," said Samuel Nathaniel Daniels, a little peeved at being told off.

Everyone watched as Bryan's HOLOGRAPHIC face REAPPEARED.

If you pay the ransom, in FULL, at the agreed time and location, then I will remain unharmed and will be freed. Freed from this secret, dark, dank room with flickering lights outside.

"There," said Compton. "THAT bit."

"*What* bit?" said The Commissioner, confused.

"The bit where he talks about the dark and dank room with flickering lights outside," said Compton. "That wasn't on the piece of paper because he wasn't looking at it when he said it. Right?"

"Er, right," said The Commissioner unconvincingly.

"So, if it wasn't on the piece of paper," said Compton, getting more excited as the pieces of the jigsaw slotted together in his mind, "he added that himself, right?"

"Er, right," said Mr Susan Glanville feebly.

"So he was giving us a clue about where he is," said Compton.

"He is in a dark, dank room with flickering lights outside. And he knows that we must know where that is, otherwise he wouldn't have said it."

"So where is it?" said Samuel Nathaniel Daniels. "It isn't like anywhere that I know."

"A dark, dank place with flickering lights? Where could Bryan be that has flickering lights?" said Compton, searching his brain for a connection – and suddenly it came to him. "Of course, it's the **F. A. R. T. Academy Test Laboratory**! It's the only place we've been to that's dark and dank and has flickering lights!"

Mr Susan Glanville looked at Compton.

"The place he used thirty years ago, of *course*!" he said, punching his hand. "Hold on, how do you know about that place? It's completely off limits."

"Ah, er, um..." said Compton, suddenly becoming **very** interested in the floor.

"Never mind about that *now*," said Samuel Nathaniel Daniels, springing into action in the hope that he wouldn't have to answer any awkward questions about *how* Compton and Bryan found out about the old abandoned corridor. "We've **got** to catch St Vincent and rescue Bryan."

The Commissioner pushed a button on her **W.A.T.CH.**

she yelled.

Chapter 27

Z99ZN8

One minute and thirty-four seconds later, the area just outside the invisible door marked,

was buzzing with activity. The Commissioner, Samuel Nathaniel Daniels, Mr Susan Glanville, Compton and twenty-five **FPU Special Agents** were all there ready to rescue Bryan.

"We go in first," said an **FPU Special Agent** from underneath his black helmet and silver visor. "Wait until you hear the signal that it is safe for you to join us."

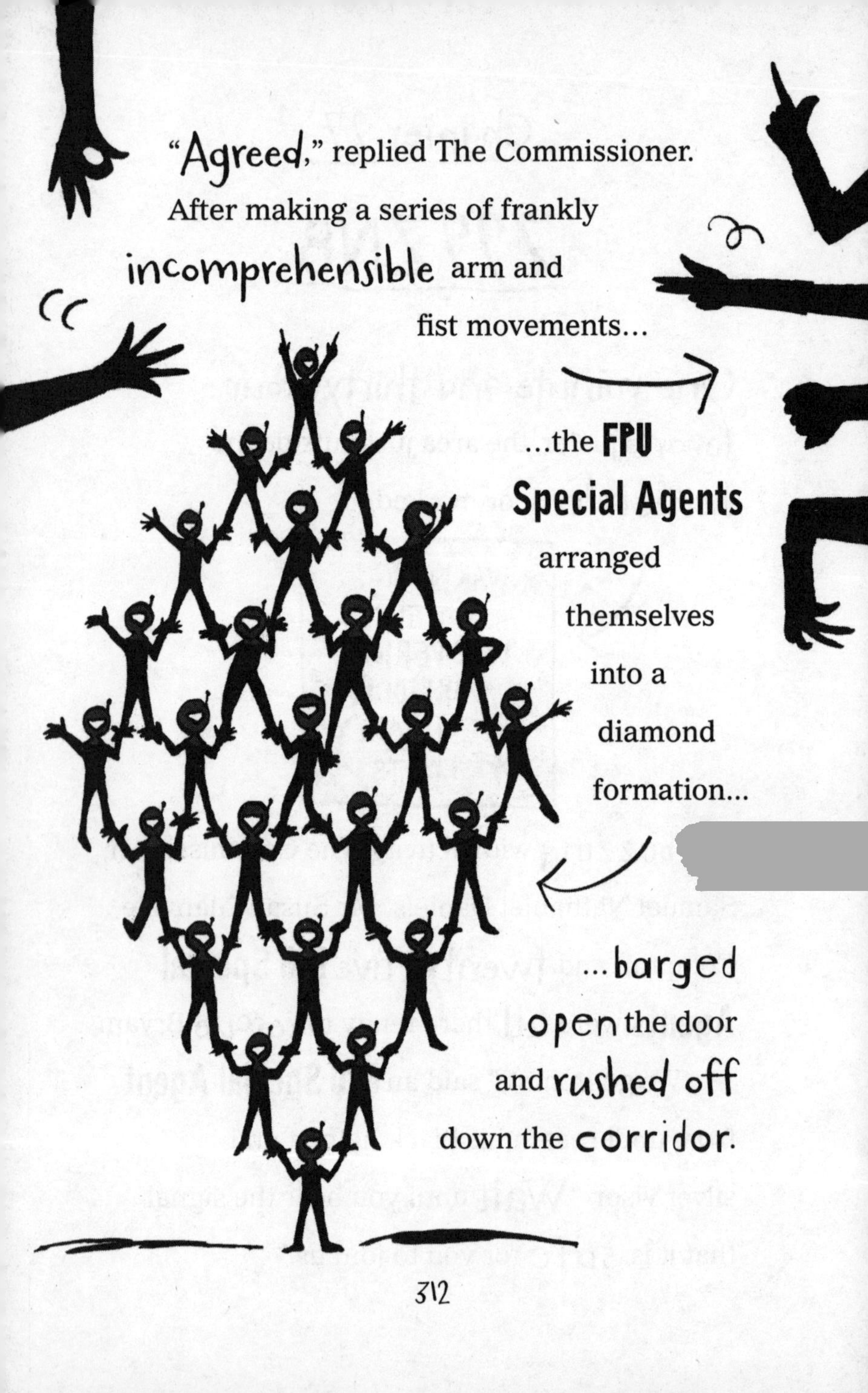
"Agreed," replied The Commissioner.

After making a series of frankly incomprehensible arm and fist movements...

...the FPU Special Agents arranged themselves into a diamond formation...

...barged open the door and rushed off down the corridor.

The Commissioner, Samuel Nathaniel Daniels, Mr Susan Glanville and Compton followed through the darkness of the corridor, their faces lit now and again by the flickering LIGHT.

Eventually they reached THE END of the corridor and peered down the staircase and into the darkness.

The Commissioner used the torch on her W.A.T.CH. to light a path through the gloom and they all went down the stairs.

"It makes perfect sense for St Vincent to use this place," said Mr Susan Glanville. "The only person who ever uses this is Ms Drimpton to occasionally walk that revolting dog of hers."

ALL CLEAR!

came the shout from along the corridor at the bottom of the stairs. Compton, Samuel Nathaniel Daniels, The Commissioner and Mr Susan Glanville all *rushed* into the **F. A. R. T. Academy Test Laboratory** at the end of the corridor.

"*Bryan?*" shouted Compton as he burst through the door.

"No one here," said an **FPU Special Agent**. "There are signs that the room has been used recently but we've just completed a DNA sweep. **Academy Agent** Nylon hasn't been here in the last 72 hours."

"*What?*" said Compton. "But that can't be. Bryan *must* be here."

"Sorry," said the **FPU Special Agent** and after a few more baffling arm and fist movements, she and the rest of the **FPU Special Agents** marched out of the room and waited outside in the corridor for further instructions.

"I just don't get it," said Compton, s l o w l y walking around the room. "This is the place, I just *know* it is."

Samuel Nathaniel Daniels put an arm round Compton's shoulder.

"Don't worry," he said kindly. "We'll find Bryan, I promise. We just need to BIDE OUR TIME."

BIDE OUR TIME BIDE OUR TIME

OUR TIME OUR TIME

TIME TIME TIME TIME TIME

The word CRASHED into Compton's brain as if it were a cricket ball that had been smashed through next door's greenhouse by a particularly miffed, bat-wielding octopus.

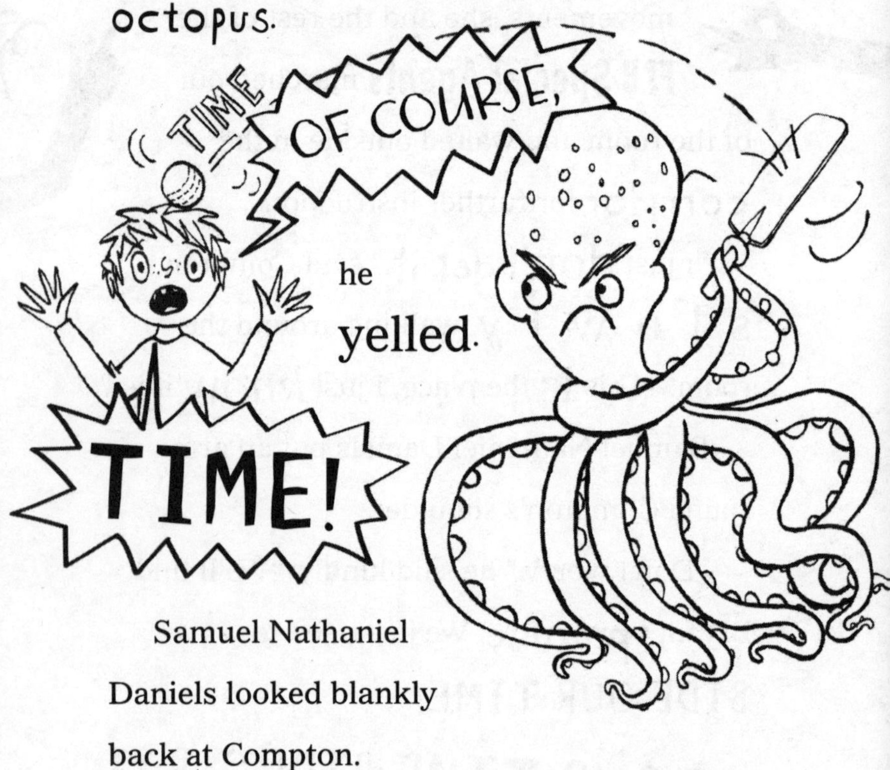

he yelled.

Samuel Nathaniel Daniels looked blankly back at Compton.

"Bryan isn't here *now*," said Compton, scanning the room quickly. "But he *was* here or will be here. I bet St Vincent has brought him here at *some* point in TIME, just not *our* point in TIME. Quick, search the room for a clue. If I know Bryan, he will have tried to send us a message."

The four of them quickly searched as *FAST* as they could.

"OVER HERE!" yelled The Commissioner. "I THINK I'VE FOUND SOMETHING."

There, in the dust, right in the corner of the room, they could see something had been scratched and *scraped* into the stone floor.

Z99ZN8

"Z99ZN8?" said Samuel Nathaniel Daniels. "What on earth does that *mean*?"

Compton thought for a moment. He was sure it must be a message from Bryan but *what* could he have been trying to say?

"Is it a room number?" offered Samuel Nathaniel Daniels.

"Or a code to unlock something?" said Mr Susan Glanville.

"It's backwards writing," said Compton suddenly. 'Like when you put 07734 into a calculator."

"*07734?*" said The Commissioner. "What are you on about?"

"Well," said Compton, "when you put the number 07734 into a calculator and turn the calculator upside down, it spells the word 'hello'."

"Oh yes," said Mr Susan Glanville. "So it does."

"So if you write Z99ZN8 upside down it says BN2662," said Compton.

"The BN bit must stand for Bryan Nylon."

"And the 2662 must be the year," said The Commissioner. "He was brought here two years ago."

"But how do we know what day to go to?" said Compton. "It could be any of them."

"Don't worry," said The Commissioner. "I'm going to send a team back to January 1st, 2662 and install a super-secret, tiny camera in the wall so that we can work out which day to go back to and rescue Bryan."

"Can't we just go back and arrest Gussage St Vincent at the same time?" said Compton.

"Oh no," said The Commissioner.

"It would mean a clear violation of the THIRD and SEVENTEENTH LAWS OF TIME," said Mr Susan Glanville icily. "Haven't you been listening to Ms Drimpton's lessons?"

The Commissioner continued. "If we go back to a time *before* Bryan left us his message and STOP St Vincent from kidnapping Bryan, then Bryan won't be able to leave his message, which means that we won't see the message, which means we won't be able to TRAVEL BACK IN TIME to rescue Bryan. It's very simple really."

And with that The Commissioner left the room to speak with the **FPU Special Agents**.

Thirty seconds later, a team of **Agents** had been sent back to January 1st, 2662 to set up a camera. Forty seconds later, The Commissioner's **W.A.T.CH.** buzzed.

"I've got a date and a time," said The Commissioner. "Let's GO." And with that she pushed some buttons on her **W.A.T.CH.**

The air in the room started to crackle and fizz, and she, Mr Susan Glanville, Samuel Nathaniel Daniels and Compton all

DISAPPEARED.

When the room stopped crackling and fizzing, Compton saw that they were in the same room again, only this time Bryan was in the corner of the room, just finishing off scratching Z99ZN8 into the floor.

"Wow," he said, standing up. "That was quick."

Compton rushed over and gave his best friend a HUGE hug.

Am I glad to see YOU,

he said.

You okay?

Bryan nodded.

"Yeah, I've only been here for twenty minutes," he said, shrugging his shoulders. "But I know *exactly* where Gussage St Vincent is going next. We've got to STOP him."

"What's he after?" asked The Commissioner. "Money? Gold? Jewels?"

"No," said Bryan, shaking his head. "A sandwich. Come on, let's go.

"The FUTURE?" said Compton.

"How *far*? Ten years?
A hundred years?
Will we get to see our own grandchildren?
Will we see a sunset formed from a thousand dying stars?"

"Unlikely," said Bryan. "We're going to go FORWARD IN TIME to 22nd August, 2664."

"Our GRADUATION DAY?" said Compton. "Why then?"

"Don't worry," said Bryan. "I'll explain everything on the way."

"Agent Daniels," said The Commissioner. "I want a FULL search made of this room. I shall leave you ten Special Agents to help. The rest will come with me and Compton and Bryan."

The Commissioner then pushed some buttons on her W.A.T.CH. and she, Compton, Bryan and fifteen Special Agents all

Chapter 28

22nd August, 2664

The Time Museum always looked wonderful on

GRADUATION DAY.

The place was full of **F. A. R. T. Academy** professors, **FPU Agents**, **Academy Agents** and the families and friends of **Academy Agents**. The whole museum was decked out with congratulatory laser displays and HOLOGRAPHIC fireworks that went off to the "ooohs" and "ahhhhs" of the assembled crowd.

Mr Susan Glanville – dressed in the traditional gold tassled Head of the F. A. R. T. Academy graduation outfit – hovered high above the audience on a large red floating disc.

"Colleagues and students," he boomed through a JENNINGS 4000 MEGAHORN. "What an afternoon it has been. Congratulations to all classes and students who have received their F. A. R. T. Academy GRADUATION CERTIFICATES so far."

The Academy Agents sitting below, wearing their gold uniforms, burst into warm, spontaneous applause.

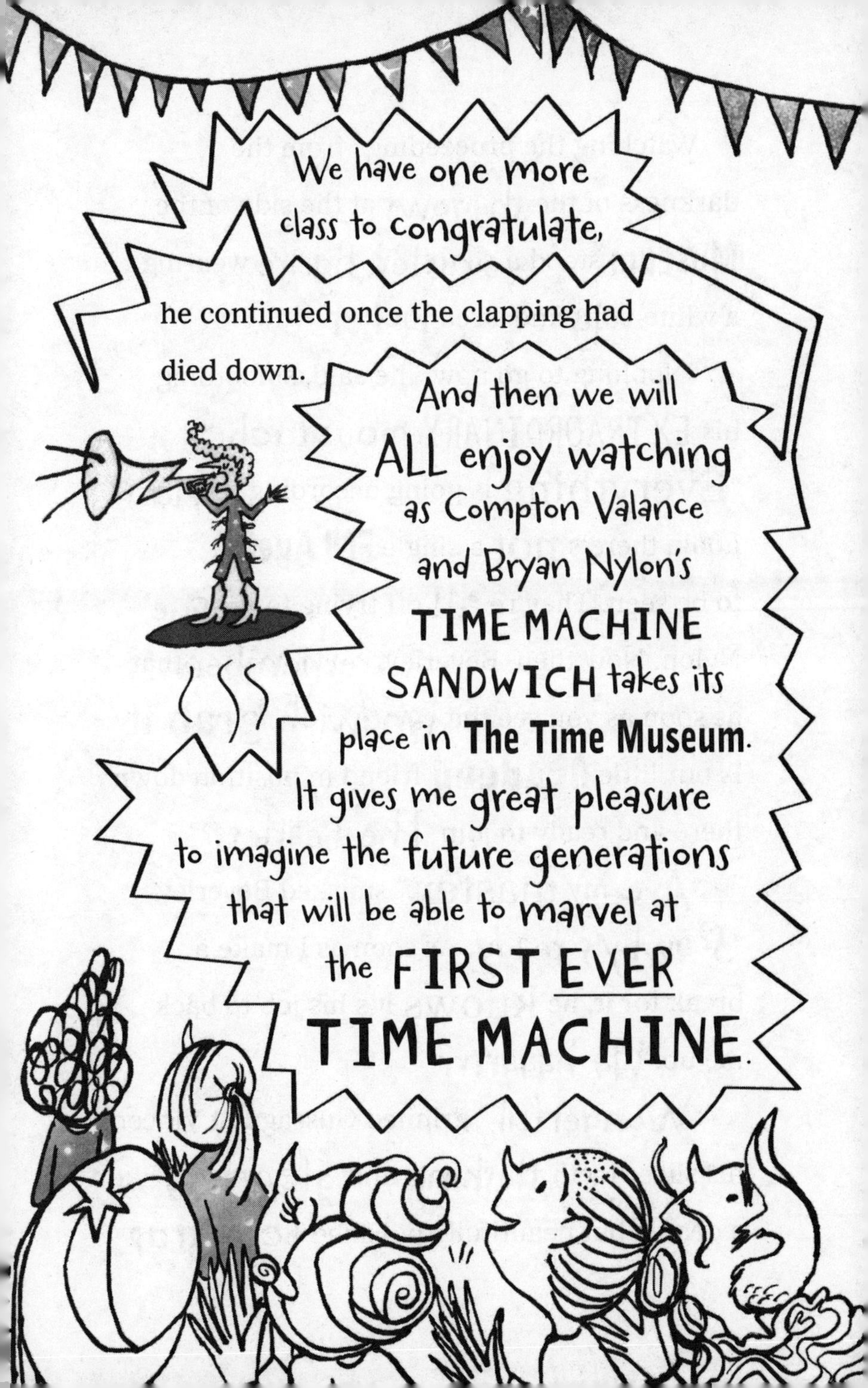

he continued once the clapping had died down.

Watching the proceedings from the darkness of the shadows at the side of the Museum stood a sinister figure wearing a white wig and a red jacket.

"Not long to go now," he said, smoothing his EXTRAORDINARY moustache. "Everything is going according to plan. Look, there's not a single FPU Agent to be seen. They're all off trying to rescue Nylon. Now then, Beverley, remember that as soon as you see the sandwich, grab it. Is our little Academy friend in position down there and ready to join The Fearless?"

"Aye, my master," smirked Beverley. "Scawby's ready. As soon as I make a break for it, he knows it's his job to back me up. Ha haaarrrr."

"Wonderful," grinned Gussage St Vincent, his silver teeth flashing and gleaming like a deadly but beautifully polished bear trap.

"We couldn't have done it without him, could we?"

"That we couldn't master," agreed Beverley. "Been our eyes and ears within the Academy he has. Had that BRILLIANT idea of hiding out in your old laboratory, didn't he? Knew no one would look for you in the Academy."

"Well quite," said Gussage St Vincent. "He managed to get me the blueprints of the Academy too and the secret access codes so that I could hack into Samuel Nathaniel Daniels's InfoTab. He'll make an excellent recruit to our little crew. Well, I mean he is family, isn't he?"

Beverley chuckled at that last remark and Gussage St Vincent drummed his fingers together with delight.

"Only a little more of this GRADUATION claptrap to go through now," he said.

"Let us give a big round of applause," continued Mr Susan Glanville, hovering above the audience, "to the PHASE ONE Academy Agents, all of whom successfully completed their BASIC TRAINING and will advance to PHASE TWO. Congratulations to Hector Wells, Lola Weena, Newton Heath, Adi Cama, Harry Stafford, Tony Chang, Scafell Nevis, Suzanne Davoise, Phil Kokinos, Ash and Mo Lyon, Tina Bizzle, Lotty Clare, Westie Dwight and Foxy Guardin."

As each PHASE ONE Academy Agent was named they stood up and bowed and the audience applauded warmly.

"And now," continued Mr Susan Glanville, "the moment you've all been waiting for!"

Suddenly, two glass cases rose out of the floor, one containing Stinky Trevor, the other EMPTY. Once the cases had finished rising, the glass surrounding the empty pedestal DISAPPEARED.

"And to bring in the TIME MACHINE SANDWICH," said Mr Susan Glanville, "please welcome our GRADUATES OF HONOUR: Compton Valance and Bryan Nylon."

Compton and Bryan, resplendent in their gold graduation uniforms, carried the sandwich into **The Time Museum** on a purple velvet cushion.

The crowd let out a gasp as they saw the sandwich for the first time. Then the crowd groaned as they caught a whiff from the sandwich as Compton and Bryan walked it s l o w l y towards the glass case.

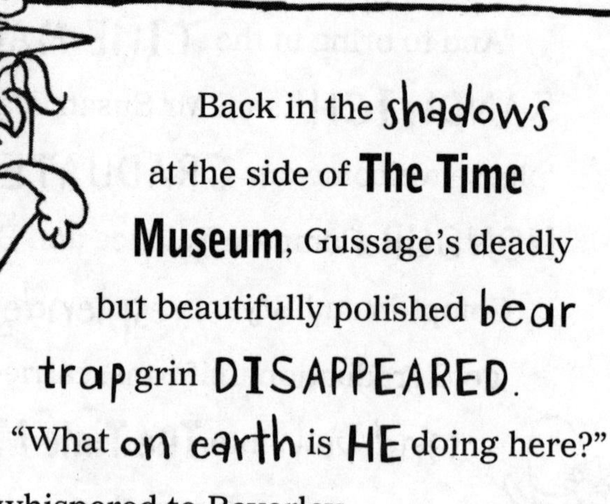

Back in the shadows at the side of **The Time Museum**, Gussage's deadly but beautifully polished bear trap grin DISAPPEARED.

"What on earth is HE doing here?" Gussage whispered to Beverley. "Bryan Nylon *should* be tied up in a secret location on the other side of New New London waiting to be rescued. *Something's* not right..."

But Beverley wasn't listening, because as soon as he saw the sandwich, he *rushed* out into the middle of the **Museum** to grab it. And *just* as Beverley made his move, Scawby Briggs leaped up from where he was sitting and *rushed* for the sandwich too.

he **yelled** waving his hands in the air.

As he did, several **FPU Special Agents** who had been hiding, **grabbed** him and Beverley and *wrestled* them to the ground.

"WHAT THE—?" yelled Gussage St Vincent from the shadows. "Why are all those Agents here? They should be trying to rescue Bryan Nylon from a secret location on the other side of New New London. What's happening?!"

"What's going on, Gussage St Vincent," said The Commissioner who had just materialized in a series of crackles and fizzes next to him, along with Compton, Bryan and fifteen more FPU Special Agents, "is that YOU are going back to prison. And this time you're not getting out."*

Without giving him any time to act,

* Okay, so just to explain what's going on. We now have two Comptons and two Bryans in the Time Museum. The Compton and Bryan who have just materialized by Gussage St Vincent are the Compton and Bryan who have just travelled from the F.A.R.T Academy Test Laboratory from two years ago. They're wearing red onesies, so I'll call them Red Compton and Red Bryan. Then we've got Gold Compton and Gold Bryan who are the future Compton and Bryans, and who are just graduating. Simple, see!

a **Special Agent** grabbed St Vincent's wrist and unclipped the stolen **W.A.T.CH.**

"B-b-but," stuttered St Vincent, barely able to comprehend what was going on.

H-h-h-how?

You CROW too much,

said Bryan.

You told me EVERY detail of your plan so that when I alerted Compton to where and when I was, it was simply a matter of catching YOU where and when you told me you'd try and steal the sandwich.

Gussage St Vincent yanked his hand away from the **FPU Agent** and smoothed down his red jacket.

"I can assure you of one thing," he said, looking straight at The Commissioner. "You won't take ME back to prison."

In one slick movement, St Vincent twisted his body around and managed to free himself from the grip of the **Special Agent** who was holding him. Then, in full view of the GRADUATION audience, he *raced* across the floor towards the glass case containing Stinky Trevor. Before the **FPU Special Agents** could do anything to STOP him, Gussage St Vincent jumped feet first at the glass case.

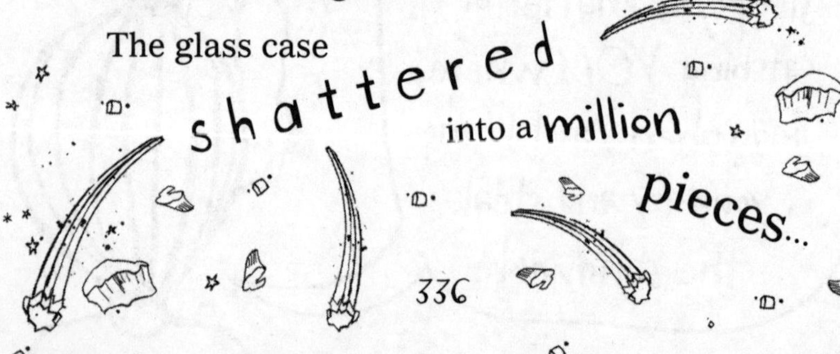

The glass case shattered into a million pieces...

and a second later, Gussage stood with his hand clasped around Stinky Trevor's beautiful golden lever. "I bid you all a good day!" he said and pulled hard.

Immediately the air around him crackled and fizzed and Gussage St Vincent

VANISHED.

The Commissioner nodded towards a **Special Agent** who pushed some buttons on his **W.A.T.C.H.** and DISAPPEARED.

"Don't panic," she said. "I've just sent back one of my best agents. They'll nab Gussage before he can get too far. That's the problem of TRAVELLING BACK IN TIME with Stinky Trevor: you can only go back twenty thousand years."

As they were waiting for the **Special Agent** to return, the air next to The Commissioner crackled and fizzed and Samuel Nathaniel Daniels APPEARED.

"We've completed the search of the **F. A. R. T. Academy test laboratory**," he said. "And we found *this*."

Samuel Nathaniel Daniels handed The Commissioner a large piece of paper. At the top of the page in elaborate writing were the names *Gussage* and *Bertha St Vincent*.

Then all the way down the page were a complicated series of lines connecting lots of other names and dates. Finally, right at the bottom of the page, was the name Scawby Briggs.

gasped The Commissioner.

Gussage St Vincent was the great, great, great, great, great, GREAT, great, great, great, great, great, GREAT, great, great, great, great, great, GREAT, great, great, great, great, great, great, GREAT, great, GREAT, GREAT GRANDFATHER of Scawby Briggs. He must have recruited Scawby when he came back two years ago. That's HOW he was able to get access to ALL the **F. A. R. T. Academy** files. It was an INSIDE JOB!

The Commissioner shook her head and looked across the **Museum**. She watched as three **FPU Special Agents** marched Scawby Briggs off to prison.

Chapter 29

The End Of Gussage St Vincent?

A few moments later, the air next to The Commissioner crackled and fizzed, and the **Special Agent**, who had been sent back twenty thousand years to catch Gussage St Vincent REAPPEARED carrying a red jacket and a blood-splattered white wig.

"I couldn't get him," he said breathlessly from underneath his helmet. "I'm afraid that he was attacked and killed by a sabre-toothed tiger. All that was left of him were these clothes."

"What a horrible way to go," The Commissioner said, looking at the wig and jacket. Then she handed the **Special Agent** the stolen **W.A.T.CH.**

she said.

Very good,
said the Special Agent.
HA HA HAAAAAAAAAA.
"I'm sorry?" said The Commissioner.
"Did you say something?"
Oh, nothing,
said the Special Agent
who began to twiddle
something on his
face underneath
his helmet as
he left.

From the shadows at the side of **The Time Museum**, Red Compton and Bryan looked over at Gold Compton and Bryan, who had just brought the TIME MACHINE SANDWICH into **The Time Museum** and who were, at that very moment, receiving their **PHASE ONE** certificates.

"Compton, I don't BELIEVE it," said Red Bryan. "It looks like you and Ms Drimpton are laughing about something."

Red Compton eyed the scene eagerly.

"Wait, my mistake," chuckled Red Bryan. "She's actually yelling at you about something."

"That's right," said Samuel Nathaniel Daniels, joining them. "And who can blame her after that incident with the cardboard box full of gravy?"*

"*Cardboard box?*" said Red Compton. "*Gravy?* What?"

"Well, you'll find out all about it for yourselves," said Samuel Nathaniel Daniels smiling warmly. "We're going to take you back to complete your PHASE ONE TRAINING."

"So we *haven't* graduated?" said Red Bryan.

* Don't ask!

"Well, the two of you who go BACK IN TIME right now, complete the TRAINING and are standing over there in your gold uniforms collecting a certificate of GRADUATION, do," said Samuel Nathaniel Daniels, smiling. And with that he pushed some buttons on his W.A.T.CH. and the air in the shadows at the side of The Time Museum

crackled and fizzed.

After a moment, Samuel Nathaniel Daniels, Red Compton and Bryan all

Across the floor, in the middle of **The Time Museum**, Gold Compton looked over at the shadows and smiled. Then he turned to Gold Bryan.

Chapter 30

Epilogue

A few moments later and anyone passing outside the F. A. R. T. Academy would have heard muffled cheers and the distant rumble of HOLOGRAPHIC fireworks echoing from inside The Time Museum. However, the streets were EMPTY and nobody was there to witness a solitary FPU Special Agent, carrying a red jacket and blood-spattered wig, bursting out of the F. A. R. T. Academy doors and into the late summer sunshine. The Special Agent <paused> for a moment and removed his helmet. He put on the red jacket he had been carrying, perched the blood-spattered wig on top of his head like an attractive bag of sugar and stroked his *unfeasibly* LARGE moustache.

Then, with a horrible smile plastered all over his chops, he placed the stolen W.A.T.CH. on his wrist and pushed some buttons. The air around him crackled and fizzed and, still holding the helmet that had concealed his true identity, GUSSAGE ST VINCENT DISAPPEARED.

Travel BACK IN TIME and read Compton and Bryan's first two eye-wateringly EXCELLENT adventures!

And, WHIZZ onwards to join Compton and Bryan on their FOURTH ASTOUNDING adventure...

COMPTON VALANCE 4

COMING SPRING 2016

Zoom over to

www.comptonvalance.com

for loads more SANDWICHES, TIME-TRAVELLING MAYHEM and SUPER-TOP-SECRET STUFF!

Acknowledgements

I would like to say here and now that this book would NOT be the crackerjack, rollercoaster ride that you have in your hands if it weren't for a load of people who helped along the way…

Firstly thank you to Liz, Joe and Sam who put up with me living in a shed for two months while I wrote the book. Thanks too, to my BRILLIANT support network of family and friends who helped out so much (Mum, Sam, Sue, Geoff, the family Gibbs, the family Hague, and Ben). Plus special thanks to Rachel for letting me use a bit of her actual real life in the book. (I shan't say which bit as it's WAY too embarrassing!) As ever, HUGE thanks go to Lizzie Finlay, the greatest artist in THE UNIVERSE, for being able to take my words and turn them into such AWESOME illustrations. Also enormous thanks to Team Usborne (Becky, Sarah, Anne, Rebecca, Neil, Hannah C, Kath, Brenda, Amy, Hannah R and Anna). You lot are truly, truly incredible human beings.

Thank you to everyone who has come to one of my events, or invited me to their school or festival. Thanks go to YOU as well for buying the book, or borrowing the book, or reading the book a page at a time in your local bookshop. Lastly (but definitely not leastly), THANK YOU to the local bookshops and the libraries in our wondrous towns and cities for all their support and kindness. They are palaces of greatness run by kings and queens and are among the finest, warmest and most beautiful places I know.

I'll stop now. THANK YOU!!!!